A Brilliant Rose

Also By Bree

Historical Romance:

<u>Love's Second Chance Series</u>
#1 Forgotten & Remembered - The Duke's Late Wife
#2 Cursed & Cherished - The Duke's Wilful Wife
#3 Despised & Desired - The Marquess' Passionate Wife
#4 Abandoned & Protected - The Marquis' Tenacious Wife

<u>A Forbidden Love Novella Series</u>
#1 The Wrong Brother
#2 A Brilliant Rose
#3 The Forgotten Wife
#4 An Unwelcome Proposal

Suspenseful Contemporary Romance:

<u>Where There's Love Series</u>
#1 Remember Me

Middle Grade Adventure:

<u>Airborne Trilogy</u>
#1 Fireflies (Now perma-free in ebook format!)
#2 Butterflies
#3 Dragonflies (Coming 2017)

Paranormal Fantasy:

<u>Crescent Rock Series</u>
#1 How to Live and Die in Crescent Rock
#2 How to Love and Hate in Crescent Rock (Coming 2018)

A Brilliant Rose

(#2 A Forbidden Love Novella Series)

by
Bree Wolf

A Brilliant Rose

by

Bree Wolf

This is a work of fiction. Names, characters, businesses, places, brands, media, events and incidents are either the products of the author's imagination or used in a fictitious manner.

Any resemblance to actual persons, living or dead, or actual events is purely coincidental.

Cover Art by Victoria Cooper

Copyright © 2016 Sabrina Wolf

www.breewolf.com

ISBN-13: 978-1534916005
ISBN-10: 1534916008

To My Dad, for Being the Grandpa We all Wish for.

Acknowledgments

A million thank-you's are not enough to express my gratitude for the loving support and understanding of my family. You are my inspiration, and I would never have published a single book without your help and encouragement!

Another big thank-you goes to Michelle Chenoweth for her willingness to read with an editor's eye, which I know is less fun than reading with a reader's eye.

And my avid readers, Zan-Mari Kiousi, Monique Takens and Tray-Ci Roberts, are the critical voices that help shape my characters and their stories in a way I could never have thought of without them. Thanks so much for your time!

A Brilliant Rose

PROLOGUE

Three Years Ago

Her heart thudding in her chest, Diana tiptoed down the small cobblestone path as her dainty steps echoed through the night air. The moon shone overhead, casting its silvery light into the shadowy dark of the gardens, and from the terrace, the sounds of music and laughter reached her ears. The earl's ball was still in full swing, and to Diana's delight, it had been rather easy to escape her parents' watchful eyes and sneak out into the night.

A part of Diana's mind warned her, cautioned her that such behaviour could have disastrous consequences. Her heart, however, was focused on one thing alone: the man she loved.

If she could only speak to him for a few moments and assure him that his pursuit was indeed most welcome, he would surely speak to her father that very night and ask for her hand in marriage.

At the thought, her breath caught in her throat, and she stopped in her tracks. Drawing the fresh night air into her lungs, Diana sought to steady her nerves. When the slight dizziness that had seized her so unexpectedly finally subsided, she swallowed and then proceeded down the path.

In the dark, the tall-growing hedges and bushes looked ominous, and more than once, Diana drew back with a startled gasp as she feared she had stumbled upon someone lurking in the shadows, intent on doing her harm.

"Where is he?" she mumbled under her breath craning her neck, hoping to catch a glimpse of his tall, striking figure.

After he had asked her to follow him into the night—the gaze in his smouldering eyes saying more than a thousand words ever could—Diana had not hesitated. Ensuring that her parents were otherwise occupied, she had slipped out the terrace doors, following his silhouette until it had disappeared among the shadows.

As the chilled night air brushed over her heated cheeks, Diana's feet carried her onward until, at last, she found the small pavilion as it stood like an island in the midst of a green ocean, its tall, white-washed pillars reaching into the sky.

Sheltered under a canopy roof, his back to her and his strong arms resting on the small rail, he stood motionless on the other side of the small space and stared out into the night.

At the very sight of him, Diana's heart soared, and a rush of emotions swept through her body. Her lips began to tingle at the mere thought of his mouth pressed to hers, and her palms grew moist with nervous anticipation.

Taking another deep breath, she stepped forward, her dainty steps all but silent as she approached him. His intoxicating scent mingled with the soft night smells as the jasmines began to bloom, and Diana thought for a moment she would faint on the spot as her heart raced in her chest.

Coming to stand behind him while desperate to be in his arms, she lifted her hands and softly placed them on the top of his back, gently letting them slide down over his strong muscles.

The moment Diana touched him, he froze...before drawing in a deep breath. "I've been waiting for you," he whispered in that deep, raspy voice that made her breath catch in her throat every time it reached her ears.

A smile spread over her face, and joy filled her heart.

Like a feline, he suddenly spun around and pulled her into his arms, his hungry mouth seeking hers.

Locked in his tight embrace, Diana abandoned all thought as her body responded to his touch as though it recognized him from a previous life. Deep down, Diana had always known that he was her soul mate.

As his lips roamed hers, she held on to him, feeling her knees grow weak. A soft gasp escaped her as his hands travelled upward, and he suddenly drew back.

In the dim light of the moon, he gazed into her eyes, a slight frown curling his brows before he stepped back. "I apologise, Miss—"

"Diana!"

At the sound of her father's enraged voice, Diana's head spun around.

Finding her parents by the tall-growing hedge that shielded the pavilion from passers-by, she swallowed as their disbelieving eyes stared at them, shifting from her to the man by her side.

A smile on her lips, Diana turned to face her parents as they hurried toward them, their own faces pale in the moonlight. "Father, Mother, I can explain."

"I most certainly hope so," her father snapped, his sharp eyes travelling from her to her future husband. "Norwood, what is the meaning of this?"

Clearing his throat, Robert Dashwood stepped forward. "I apologise, sir. There has been some misunderstanding. I—"

"Whatever misunderstanding you thought has occurred, I expect the next words I hear to include a proposal considering the liberties you've just now taken with my daughter!"

With love in her heart and a smile on her face, Diana turned to the man by her side. Butterflies fluttered in her belly as she took a deep breath. *This was it! The moment she had been waiting for her entire life.*

"A proposal?" Laughing, her soul mate shook his head. "I'm afraid I have to disappoint you."

Staring at him, Diana felt the blood rush from her cheeks as the world grew dim around her. "What?" she gasped, her knees suddenly as weak as pudding as the butterflies in her belly died a slow death.

"I apologise," he said, his eyes shifting from her father to her. "As I said, this was a misunderstanding."

"A misunderstanding?" her father boomed as heart-wrenching sobs tore from Diana's throat, and she sank into her mother's arms.

"You take advantage of a young girl and then you refuse to do the only decent thing there is left. What kind of a gentleman are you?"

Chuckling, Lord Norwood leaned against the rail. "The worst kind, I assure you."

"Social etiquette dictates that—"

"I don't care about social etiquette—"

"You will be ruined. Your reputation—"

"My reputation will not suffer, for all of London already knows the kind of man I am." Standing up straight, the notorious viscount stepped forward, fixing her father with serious eyes. "Your daughter, on the other hand, has everything to lose. Therefore, I suggest you be reasonable."

"You downright refuse to marry her?" her father huffed.

"Yes, sir," he confirmed. "You will be well-advised to return to the festivities before we are discovered. No harm has been done so far."

Shaking his head, her father coughed, "No harm? You've compromised her."

"Upon my honour—or what is left of it—it was only a kiss."

Only a kiss? Diana's head spun as she clung to her mother, her hopes crashing into a black abyss that was threatening to swallow her whole. What was happening? Did he not love her? Had he not told her so a million times? Had his loving gaze not spoken the words that his lips had confirmed a mere few minutes ago?

Glaring at the man she loved, her father returned to her side. "You are without honour, Norwood. I sincerely hope that one day you will reap what you sow."

An amused smile on his face, Lord Norwood nodded to her father before his eyes dropped to hers. "All my best to you, Miss…Lawson, is it?" Then he turned and walked away, the shadows swallowing him whole as though he had never been there.

Supported by a parent on either side, Diana placed one step before the other, her mind tormented by the incomprehensibility of what had just happened and her heart aching with the love so unexpectedly ripped from her life.

"I can only hope that Norwood keeps quiet," her father mumbled under his breath, anger still ringing in his sharp voice. "If anyone finds out what happened here tonight, your chances of a favourable match will be ruined."

In that moment, Diana could not bring herself to care. After all, what value could her reputation possibly have when her heart had just been ripped into pieces?

1

IN HIS BROTHER'S SHOES

England 1818 (or a variation thereof)

As the new year began, Bridgemoore found itself covered in a soft layer of snow. The sky gleamed a clear blue dotted with white clouds, and the sun shone brightly, its golden rays reflected in the millions of ice crystals that clung to the frozen ground.

Blinking, Charles Dashwood stepped back from the tall window in his study as the blinding light reached his eyes.

Only the day before, dark clouds had loomed high above the estate like a bad omen for the new year to come. Never would he have expected such a change, and yet, it resonated deep within him.

The old year had ended in a tragedy as Princess Charlotte's death in childbirth as well as the loss of her son had plunged the whole nation into mourning. Black dominated every area of life as people felt the need to express their sorrow. Charles, too, had received the news with a heavy heart.

After losing his own mother early and rather unexpectedly, he was acutely aware of how fragile life could be. Within an instant, the happiness of a moment ago could lie shattered at one's feet. This knowledge had often cautioned him when it came to matters of the heart. Rarely had Charles opened himself up to another human being and the risk of heartache such an action could entail. Only his older twin did he love without restriction.

Months had passed since he had last seen Robert as he and his new bride Isabella had embarked on an adventure that led them around the world. Last he'd heard, they were in Italy.

With a smile on his face, Charles glanced at the tall stack of letters neatly set aside on his desk. Although the two brothers had drifted apart the years prior to the wedding, now they were inseparable as ever—despite the distance that currently lay between them. Rarely a week passed without a new letter from Robert, and Charles could not help but look forward to the day that his brother would return to Bridgemoore.

Once again, his eyes shifted to the powdered world at his feet, stretching to the far horizon, the snow's pure white fading into the sparkling blue of the sky. The world did, indeed, look different that morning—promising—and Charles felt a slight flip in his stomach, hoping that the new year would not fall short of the promises that echoed in his heart that day.

As a knock on the door tore him from his musings, Charles straightened. "Enter," he called and returned to his desk.

With a slightly hesitant step, Mr. Hill walked into the study. "Good morning, my lord."

"Good morning," Charles replied as his steward's unfamiliar address rang in his ears. Although months had passed since he and his brother had switched their identities, which had resulted in Charles' promotion to the rank of a viscount, his mind still stumbled over the undue address, and he could not help but wonder if they had made a mistake.

However, whenever he remembered his brother's glowing eyes as he had looked upon Isabella with love so evident in them, all doubts were dispersed.

Never had he seen two people so much in love, and although Charles cared deeply for Isabella, she was merely a friend to him, a good friend. After all, he had not proposed to her out of love but because they were suited to each other, and she had accepted his proposal for the very same reason. How were they to know that

Isabella would find her one true love upon meeting his brother…after she had spoken her marriage vows to Charles?

The only solution to their unfortunate love triangle had been to trade their lives and everything that entailed.

So far, everything had gone smoothly. The past few months at Bridgemoore had passed in mostly the same fashion as before. Despite the fact that Robert as the elder had inherited the title, Charles had always taken care of the estate while his brother had travelled the world, always seeking new adventures. Therefore, Charles simply continued his old routines and dealt with tenants, the upkeep of the estate as well as social responsibilities as he always had.

Only now, he would sign his brother's name; and people would address him as Lord Norwood.

"The repairs to the roof in the east wing are finished, my lord," Mr. Hill, a young man in his mid-twenties, informed him. Although they had been working side by side for the past five years, Mr. Hill now appeared somewhat hesitant and reserved around him, and Charles had to remind himself again and again that the man thought him to be his brother, which would attest to his obvious anxiety. "Now, the wallpaper and furnishings will be replaced as soon as possible." A murderous storm had rolled through the county a few days ago, and a bolt of lightning had almost set the roof aflame. However, the small fire had been quickly extinguished by the torrents of rain pouring from the heavens, only leaving behind a hole in the roof and a soaking wet guest room.

"Thank you," Charles replied, an encouraging smile on his face. "However, there is no rush since the room will not be in use any time soon." He liked Mr. Hill and hoped that the man's unease caused by Robert's rather wild reputation would eventually be soothed through continued respect and civility. "Besides, I will travel to London within a fortnight," he nodded to Mr. Hill, "and will leave the upkeep of Bridgemoore in your capable hands."

A shy smile flitted over the man's face. "Yes, my lord."

"Is that all?"

"Yes, my lord."

"Good," Charles nodded, and once more his eyes shifted to the tall stack of letters. "I would ask you to forward any letters from my brother or his wife that arrive during my absence to my London townhouse immediately."

"I will, my lord," Mr. Hill assured him, his head bobbing up and down. "I will see to everything."

"Thank you," Charles said, noticing with relief that the strain on the young man's face had lessened during their conversation. He could only hope that his absence for the Season would not nourish it once more.

On his way into London, Charles found himself captivated by the dynamic city once again. Ever since his father had taken him into Town over a decade ago to see the Rosetta Stone at the British Museum, he had been taken with the vibrancy that seemed to echo off each and every brick. The streets hummed with the sounds of carts and carriages, hoof beats and voices of animals and people alike, and yet, a serenity hung over the city as though nothing could ever disrupt the rhythm of its existence.

Despite a sense of fatigue that settled on his limbs from the long journey, Charles felt rejuvenated by the city's life force pulsing through his veins. As they drove by Somerset House where the Royal Society was housed, he spotted two old friends from Eton. Delighted, he was about to rap on the roof and ask the coachman to stop when he realised that he was no longer Charles Dashwood.

Sighing, Charles dropped his hand, watching his former friends climb the steps to the front door and vanish inside as his carriage drove by.

By relinquishing his name and identity, he had not only 'gained' his brother's scandalous reputation, but he had also lost his own place in life. No longer was he a member of the Royal Society or the Society of Antiquaries. No longer could he walk up to old friends and discuss the newest developments in all areas of science. No longer could he expect to be taken seriously when voicing his opinion in public.

For years, Charles had observed how people treated or rather thought about his brother. Although few actually disliked him, his reputation for disregarding social etiquette whenever fancy struck him often made him look like a rebellious youth, who simply didn't know any better. On top of that, his boyish charm enchanted and beguiled; however, it also enforced the ton's general impression that he should not be taken seriously. Were it not for his random love affairs, most people would probably shake their heads at him, an indulgent smile on their faces.

As he climbed the steps to his townhouse, Charles wondered what this Season would bring. Since he was no longer considered a member, he could not possibly spend his time at the Society of Antiquaries, and even though Lord Norwood received an invitation to most events, who would he speak to? More importantly, who would speak to him? And what about?

Shaking his head, Charles sank into the heavy armchair in the back drawing room. Although Robert and he had shared as much of their previous lives with each other before the happy couple had embarked on their journey, Charles felt completely unprepared for the task at hand. How was he to make everyone believe he was his brother? And even if he could, would London be the happy place it had always been for him?

Fortunately, Robert had been abroad the past two years. Therefore, Charles hoped that no recent issues would arise from his brother's past to torment him today.

After a few days of carefully reacquainting himself with the city, Charles found himself in his carriage one night as it slowly made its way to the townhouse of the Earl of Tanwilth. The earl's eldest daughter was to enjoy her first Season this year, and her father obviously intended to provide her with ample opportunity to meet eligible bachelors.

Somewhat startled at the thought, Charles realised that he, too, would be considered an eligible bachelor. Despite his marriage to Isabella, by taking on his brother's identity, he had effectively become a free man once again.

Remembering the way mothers generally eyed Robert with caution and carefully watched their innocent daughters, lest he succeed in seducing them without proposing marriage, Charles wondered if he would ever find a woman that would not only suit him but whose parents would also allow him within speaking distance of her.

Chuckling at the absurdity of the situation he suddenly found himself in, Charles entered the ballroom, his eyes sweeping the many guests in attendance. While he recognised most faces, there were a few he had once counted among his friends.

Of their own accord, his feet moved toward Lord Neswold, an old friend with whom he had shared many an interesting conversation about the three texts inscribed on the Rosetta Stone.

As Charles approached, Neswold turned to him, his eyes

narrowed as they slid over his appearance. The good-humoured smile vanished from his face, and he straightened his shoulders. "Norwood."

Taking a deep breath, Charles inclined his head in greeting. "Good evening, it is a splendid night, is it not?"

"It would appear so," Lord Neswold mumbled, clearly wondering why in the world Charles—or rather Robert—was speaking to him. "Have you heard from your brother?" he asked after a moment of uncomfortable silence.

"I have, indeed," Charles said, grateful to have something to say. "He and his wife are currently travelling through Italy."

"That sounds marvellous," Neswold said, and the stern look on his face softened. "Your brother is a good man, and I am glad he is taking this time to enjoy himself."

A self-conscious smile curled up Charles' lips. "He is, thank you."

"I look forward to seeing him upon his return."

Charles nodded and took his leave, sensing that they had reached the end of their conversation.

Fortunately, people seemed to have no doubt that he was, indeed, Viscount Norwood, and, therefore, their secret was not in danger of being revealed. However, Charles could not help but feel a sense of loss, and although he was glad that there was no one at this ball, who had spoken to his brother in the last two years, he wondered how to pass his time that night.

Ultimately, Charles found himself wandering from room to room, exchanging a few pleasantries and greeting people here and there. However, when he tried to speak to old friends of his, the short dialogue that ensued always continued down the same path as the one with Lord Neswold.

Feeling disheartened, Charles returned to the refreshment table, procuring himself a glass of wine. As he stood to the side, watching the happy couples dance the night away to the lively tune played by the orchestra, he wondered about the value of friendship. How differently would this night have gone had he been able to reveal his true self!

"Tonight proves to be a marvellous start into the Season."

Almost choking on his drink, Charles turned in surprise. "Mr. Lawson, it is good to see you!" he beamed, beyond himself with joy that someone would seek his company.

Mr. Lawson, a middle-aged man with laughing eyes, frowned at his reply, and Charles swallowed. "I have to admit I didn't expect you to remember me. After all, it has been years since your father introduced his young boys to me."

"It has," Charles mumbled, searching for an explanation.

Mr. Lawson, however, grinned at him. "Your father always wondered what it would take for you to return to Town."

Charles swallowed, knowing that this was dangerous terrain. Mr. Lawson had been a treasured acquaintance of his father's, and over the years, Charles, too, had shared the occasional conversation with him. After all, Mr. Lawson had spent the previous thirty years working on historical artefacts, such as the Rosetta Stone.

Only too well did Charles remember the spring that he had been introduced to Mr. Lawson. A million questions had flown out of his mouth about the ancient texts chiselled into the stone and their importance for deciphering Egyptian hieroglyphs. Robert, on the other hand, had been bored out of his mind and had voiced his displeasure in his usual frank manner.

Their father had not been pleased.

"I apologise for my inappropriate behaviour back then," Charles said, finding it odd to apologise for something he hadn't done. "I ought not to have spoken as I did."

Laughing, Mr. Lawson waved his apology away. "To be frank, your behaviour was quite within the norm. Few boys that age have an interest in these matters. Your brother was the rare exception."

A delighted smile came to Charles' face. "My…our father always spoke to me…eh…him about the longevity of the world and the small steps its people take on the way to understanding its secrets. It's always fascinated me…I mean, him." Cursing himself, Charles tried to ignore the slightly confused expression on Mr. Lawson's face. "Charles often spoke to me about the marvels of the universe."

Mr. Lawson nodded. "I remember him fondly and was pleased to hear he has found a wife to share these interests. From what I heard, the new Mrs. Dashwood has quite a historical mind herself."

"She does," Charles agreed, mourning the loss of his companion, who had often enriched these nights with her sharp wit. "I believe them to be an excellent match. They are currently travelling the world, for Isabella was quite in raptures about seeing some of the sights she had been reading about with her own eyes."

"I should imagine so," Mr. Lawson said. "I, myself, have always enjoyed travel. It allows us to put the artefacts we discover in a proper context. However, the diligent study of these artefacts is my true passion." He smiled apologetically, and Charles delighted in the childish gleam that came to his eyes. "The secrets they unearth are the very reason I…" He stopped and shook his head as though at himself. "I apologise. I do not mean to bore you with these matters."

Honestly interested, Charles stepped forward. "Not at all. I am eager to hear what you have to say."

Mr. Lawson smiled at him indulgently, and Charles felt reminded of his brother. "Your manners have, indeed, improved," Mr. Lawson chuckled. "If I didn't know any better, I'd believe you to be a dedicated student of the ancient world. However, I do know better, and, therefore, I insist you leave my rather tedious company and join conversations more suited to your interests."

Patting him on the shoulder, Mr. Lawson turned to leave. "It has been a pleasure speaking with you. Next time, I will introduce you to my daughter. Although knowing her as I do, you will probably find her similarly tedious." Laughing, Mr. Lawson returned to the circle of colleagues to which Charles no longer enjoyed the privilege of being acquainted.

Remaining behind, Charles wondered if there was a way for him to openly show interest in the sciences without arousing suspicions. What would people think if he suddenly expressed an interest of joining the Society of Antiquaries?

Sighing, Charles procured himself another drink.

Tomorrow, he would visit the British Museum. That, at the very least, no one could deny him.

2

LOYALTY

ipping her tea, Rose glanced at her father. Hidden behind *The Times*, he occasionally reached for his muffin or teacup before returning to the words on the page.

Rose cleared her throat, possibly a little too vehemently.

Mr. Lawson, however, as he was completely absorbed in the news of the day, ignored her.

Her lips thinned, and her eyes narrowed. Then she set down her teacup with such force that for a second she feared the saucer had broken.

Lowering the right half of the newspaper, her father glanced at her through squinted eyes. "Would it not be easier to voice your objections verbally, my dear?" The hint of a grin tickled his lips. "If you continue to destroy our good china in order to get my attention, what will we drink from in the future?"

Rolling her eyes, Rose shook her head. "As always you're exaggerating, Father. It was one teacup."

"And one saucer if I recall correctly." Setting down the paper, her father turned to her, a twinkle in his eyes and a mischievous grin on his face.

Some days, Rose swore he was a young boy trapped in an old man's body!

A scientist at heart, her father had married late in life as no woman could compete with his one true love. Only after her mother had died in childbirth had Mr. Lawson realised that there was an even greater miracle in his life than the study of ancient societies. From the moment the midwife had laid Rose in his arms, he had doted on her as any devoted father would.

As far as Rose could remember, they had never spent a day apart. Unlike other fathers, he had never felt the need to appear too respectable. Crawling around in her nursery on all fours with her on his back, they had spent many a wonderful day. He had taught her to read and write and opened up his world to her without hesitation, delighted with her hungry mind and quick wit. Many days, Rose had accompanied him in his work, learning Latin and Greek, hoping to understand the few remnants left by societies past. Their conversations had always been a source of joy for her because only in her father's company did Rose feel truly accepted for who she was.

"What can I do for you, my dear?" he asked, his eyes earnest as they searched her face. "You seem distraught."

"I am." Taking a deep breath, Rose met her father's gaze. "I am worried about Diana."

Rolling his eyes, her father huffed something unintelligible before picking up his newspaper once again.

Frowning, Rose stared at him. "How can you not care about her misery? She is your niece, after all."

"What misery?" Dropping the paper, her father shook his head as red blotches crawled up his face. He took a deep breath, trying to remain calm. "I love her dearly, but that girl is a spoiled chit!"

Rose's mouth fell open.

"I mean no disrespect," her father continued before she could object, "but as an only child, she has always gotten whatever she wanted, and she expects no less of the world."

"I am an only child as well," Rose pointed out. "Do I dare ask what you think of me?"

For a moment, her father stared at her, then the agitation left his face, and he reached out, gently placing his hand on hers. "My dear

Rose, maybe you are right not to blame her for her faults because, after all, it was her parents who indulged her every whim and turned her into the woman she is today."

Rose knew his words to be true. As the firstborn son, her uncle had inherited the title of a baron as well as the family estate and its financial resources. When after a number of miscarriages, Diana had been born, both, he and his wife, had been overjoyed, spoiling her to no ends. As a result, Diana had turned into a spoiled chit—as her father had called her—demanding that everything was carried out precisely as she desired.

However, Rose also knew—while her father did not—the very reason why Diana's life had suddenly become such a burden to her.

Meeting her father's caring eyes, Rose knew that she could never reveal to him her cousin's secret as Diana had sworn her to secrecy.

Her father nodded, and the hint of a smile lit up his face. "However, I am guilty of the same transgression, and yet, you have become a woman who makes me proud every day."

Not only his words, but also the love that shone in his eyes brought tears to her own, and a deep smile came to her face. "Thank you, Father."

"Don't thank me," he said, patting her hand. "I suppose it is not because of my influence, but rather in spite of it, that you turned into such a marvellous, young woman," he chuckled. "However, I fear that London society will never know considering that you missed your first ball last night. I thought you were at least somewhat excited about your first Season in Town."

"I am," Rose assured him. "However, Diana needed me, and I could not leave her."

Rolling his eyes once again, her father shook his head. "Did she not just have a baby?" he asked. "I thought women enjoyed motherhood. What could she possibly be complaining about now?"

"Women are not solely on this earth to be mothers," Rose snapped, wondering where that hint of anger had come from.

Not offended in the least, her father grinned, patting her hand once again. "I apologise if I have offended your sensitivities, my dear. I know very well—"

"I wish you wouldn't treat me like a delicate flower," Rose interrupted. "Say what you have to say, and do not apologise for it."

"As you wish, my dear Rose." A mischievous gleam came to his eyes as he chuckled into his beard. "What I meant to say—before you

26

so rudely interrupted me—was that I know very well how capable women are. After all, I have you to remind me of that every day."

"Thank you," Rose mumbled, a slight blush colouring her cheeks as she regretted her rather inappropriate outburst.

"If I am not to apologise, then you are not to thank me." Her father held out his hand to her. "Do we have an agreement?"

A smile on her face, she took his hand.

"Promise me you will do something entertaining today," her father said. "Spending your days listening to your cousin's imagined complaints cannot be good for your health." He glanced at the paper, then met her eyes again. "How about a visit to the British Museum? That place always brings the most wonderful glow to your eyes."

Rose nodded. "That is a splendid idea, Father."

"I wish you wouldn't sound so surprised!"

Chuckling, Rose reached for her teacup. "I will go and ask Diana if she wants to accompany me."

Dropping the paper, her father stared at her. "That is not what I had in mind. Do you misunderstand me on purpose?"

"No, not at all. However, you are right. Diana needs to get out for a little while and do something enjoyable. Maybe it will lift her spirits."

Folding the paper, her father leaned forward, resting his forearms on the table. "First, I was talking about you, not Diana. Second, as far as I know, that girl cares very little for artefacts of any kind."

Rose shrugged. "Maybe I can change her mind."

Shaking his head, her father chuckled. "Learn to recognise a lost battle, my dear. It will save you heartbreak and disappointment." Before Rose could object, he lifted a hand to stop her. "Since I know my niece—and I know she'll have no interest in cultivating her knowledge on ancient societies—I shall stop by her townhouse around noon and escort you to the museum myself, thereby ensuring that you will not spend the whole day catering to Diana's every need." Her father's eyes narrowed as he regarded her. "Or do you have any objections?"

Rose shook her head. "I do not, Father. Thank you, for I truly wish to see the stone again."

Although only two years Rose's senior, Diana deported herself like an old woman whenever her *imagined complaints*—as Rose's father called them—plagued her. Whining and wailing, she moved from the settee to the armchair and back again, a moist handkerchief draped over her forehead so as to soothe the migraine that had assailed her once again. Whenever her spirits were low, she was a nightmare to be around, and yet, Rose could not help but pity her for the losses she had suffered.

"Maybe you should return to your bedchamber," Rose suggested, suspiciously eyeing the brilliant sunlight reaching inside the drawing room through the wide-open curtains. "The dark will ease the pain and allow you to rest."

"Rest?" Diana shrieked, her head jerking off the backrest of the armchair. "I would rather die than spend another day locked up in that room, all alone in the dark."

Rose sighed. Her cousin's fits of melodramatic exaggeration exhausted her. "You were not locked up, Diana. You were in childbed," she reminded her, hoping that the thought of her new-born son would bring a smile to her face.

It did not.

"Dear Cousin, if you knew what childbirth meant," Diana spat, "you would not speak of it as though it were a delight." Sinking back into the armchair, she closed her eyes.

"You are right," Rose conceded. "I do not know. However, your son is born now. Do you not delight in his presence?" Remembering the sweet, little boy, a wistful smile came to Rose's lips. "Is he not a blessing?"

"A blessing?" her cousin echoed, incomprehension ringing in her voice as she met Rose's gaze. "How could he be? He only reminds me of the man I was forced to marry."

Sitting down across from her cousin, Rose looked deep into Diana's eyes, hoping that her cousin would listen to the words she needed to hear. "I feel for you, Diana. I truly do," Rose said, and relief washed over her when her cousin's features softened. "I know how ill you were treated and how that forced you down a road you would not have chosen for yourself. However," reaching out, she grasped her cousin's hand, "what is done is done. You cannot change the past. Are you willing to sacrifice your future for a man who only treated you with disregard?"

Tears streamed down Diana's face. "It was just one night. One foolish night, and now I live with regret every day."

"I know."

"I should never have trusted him," Diana whispered, wiping the moist handkerchief over her flushed face. "I know the words you speak are true, dear Cousin. However, it is easier said than done."

"Why?" Rose asked, afraid that the moment of honest reflection would slip from her grasp. How many times had she pleaded with Diana to leave the past behind? Countless times. Wallowing in her pain, her cousin had never listened, never understood a word Rose had said. "It is only your own pain and regret that keep you from moving forward."

Diana took a deep breath, then she closed her eyes and shook her head. "It is not." Meeting Rose's gaze, she sat up. "I hear he has returned to Town." Rose swallowed. "How am I to walk with my head held high when the whispers will start anew now that he is back?"

"I didn't know," Rose admitted, suddenly feeling defeated. "When did he arrive back in Town?"

"From what I heard he returned to England for his brother's wedding and has spent the last few months at his family's estate." She met Rose's eyes then, deep pain only too visible in them. "He has been in London these two weeks past."

Rose looked at her cousin through narrowed eyes, and what she saw whipped the air from her lungs. Despite everything that had happened, Diana still cared for the man who had broken her heart. If he were to call on her, she would not be able to send him away.

Rose shivered at the thought.

A baby's cries echoed through the halls, and Diana squeezed her eyes shut. "He has been doing this all night!"

"He needs you," Rose reminded her, feeling her own heart go out to the helpless infant. Why was it that Diana was immune to the needs of her own son? "You are his mother. Go to him."

"I have a nursemaid for that," Diana objected, shaking her head determinedly.

"You need him, too," Rose insisted. "He is the only one who can heal your heart."

Diana snorted. "Puh! He is his father's son. And such an awful name...Benedict." She shook herself as though ill. "That silly family tradition of giving the first born son his father's middle name. Ugh! He will never find a wife with that name. Just like his father, there is nothing appealing about him. Despite his fortune, no woman in her right mind would ever have agreed to marry him." Closing her eyes, Diana sighed. "Neither would I. Only I didn't have a choice."

"Come outside with me," Rose urged her. "It is not good for you to spend all your time indoors, regretting what was." A tentative smile came to Diana's face. "I promised my father to go to the British Museum today; come with me!"

Diana slumped back in her chair. "Go without me. The last thing I need right now is a stuffy museum. In all honesty, I cannot understand what makes you enjoy it so." Closing her eyes, she draped the handkerchief back over her eyes while her son's cries echoed from the second floor.

3

A KINDRED SOUL

Ascending the first two stairs to Montagu House, Rose lifted her head and gazed up at the stately manor that housed the British Museum. Under its roof, large collections of artefacts had found their final resting place, and whenever Rose set foot over its threshold, a chill went down her back as though these artefacts were not soulless objects but filled with the spirits of times past, eager to share their secrets with her.

"Ah! There it is," her father exclaimed, and Rose turned her head to look at him.

"There is what?"

"The glowing smile that rivals the sun," he said, his eyes sweeping over her in unadulterated happiness. "I shall be back shortly. Enjoy yourself! However, I have no doubt that you will."

"Thank you, Father, for not saying *I told you so.*"

Suppressing a grin, he nodded. "I would never dream of it."

After being admitted, she ventured through the lower floor, awed by the large library, its rows upon rows of books filling the walls on all sides of her. If she only had the time to read them all! She mused, *What would it feel like to possess the knowledge gathered in these volumes? What wisdom would they bring?*

Heading upstairs, Rose ran her eyes over the various modern works of art located on the upper floor, and while she appreciated their unique essence, her feet were irrevocably drawn to the gallery.

Not once did her gaze travel to the other visitors, who were engrossed in the artefacts on display just as much as her. Their hushed voices and quiet footsteps mingled into a soft melody that soothed her rattled mind and comforted her aching heart.

Approaching the gallery, everything fell away, and for one pure moment, Rose felt liberated of the burdens that plagued her.

Feasting her eyes on the sight before her, Rose sighed. The gallery was by far her most favourite place in the world!

Beautifully crafted terra cottas, drawings and engravings lined the walls, and Greek and Roman sculptures decorated the room, hinting at societies long gone while Sir William Hamilton's collection of Greek vases allowed for a rare view of ancient life.

"Beautiful," Rose whispered as her mind absorbed the small details of various illustrations, guessing at their importance, at their meaning for the world today.

Lost in her own musings, Rose suddenly found herself standing in the one spot that held her heart. Without conscious thought, her feet would always direct her here as though it called to her. Lifting her head, she gazed almost lovingly at the Rosetta Stone.

A large, black granite rock, it held a decree issued in the times of the Pharaohs in Ancient Egypt. What was unusual was that the decree was written in three scripts: Ancient Egyptian hieroglyphs, Demotic script and Ancient Greek. However, so far no one had been able to decipher every last one of the words written there; the Ancient Egyptian hieroglyphs posed a problem.

Marvelling at the fine line between knowing and not knowing, Rose smiled, whispering her father's favourite Greek quote, "Εν οίδα ότι ουδέν οίδα." It seemed appropriate considering the vastness of yet undiscovered knowledge.

"I know one thing that I know nothing," a deep and rather surprised sounding voice spoke out behind her, and Rose spun around, startled.

Wide-eyed, she jerked up her head and stared at the tall man standing before her as his eyes shifted from the stone to meet hers, a delighted twinkle in them. Strong with broad shoulders, he towered above her. His gentle features, though, spoke of a kind and honest man, and Rose exhaled the breath she had been holding.

His gaze held hers, and an enchanting smile curled up his lips. "I have never before met a woman who could quote Socrates and in Ancient Greek, too."

As the honest admiration in his words resonated within her, Rose found herself swept away by his deep hazel eyes which looked into hers as though she herself were a rare artefact.

Feeling suddenly flustered, Rose averted her gaze; after all, it was not proper to stare at a stranger. "It is my father's favourite saying," she explained, grateful to have something to say. "He feels the lack of knowledge is its own greatest asset as it motivates us to understand what we do not know."

His brows rose into arches as he nodded his head. "I suppose few people would consider lack of knowledge a desirable state. However, I do see the wisdom in your father's words. He, himself, must be a man of great knowledge to have come to that conclusion."

Rose chuckled, "I do believe so. However, my father would not agree with your judgement of him."

Instead of surprise, understanding curled up the corners of his mouth. "He would not? Would you say it is modesty which keeps him from admitting to the wisdom he possesses? Or rather the desire to lower the expectations of others?"

Feeling herself smile up at him openly, Rose cleared her throat. "While my father claims that he does not know nearly enough to be called wise, in my opinion, he is merely afraid to disappoint, yes." Delighted with their conversation, Rose searched her mind for something else to say. Never before had a man besides her father spoken to her as though her mind was equal to his.

As she looked at this stranger, who had appeared out of nowhere, she saw no hint of superiority or condescension in his eyes. Instead, she saw the same desire to understand, to gain knowledge and to see the world for all its possibilities.

Where had this man been all her life?

As his feet carried him up the stairs and toward the gallery, Charles felt as though he were coming home. Although the museum had acquired new artefacts since the last time he had visited, the Rosetta Stone called to him.

When his father had taken him to London that first summer, the visit to the British Museum had marked Charles's first steps into the historical societies that had been his home these past ten years. Back then, it had been this ancient stone, newly arrived from Egypt, that had drawn visitors from far and near, and to this day, to Charles, it was the embodiment of the possibilities of ancient knowledge.

However, as he approached the stone, he found his usual spot occupied by a young woman of medium height. Her golden-red hair rested softly on her slender shoulders as her eyes swept almost lovingly over the finely chiselled inscriptions. Something about the way she held her head slightly bowed, her hands linked as though in prayer, spoke to him, and he drew near.

Debating what to do, he stood behind her right shoulder for a short while as his eyes went back and forth between her and the stone.

Then a soft smile touched her lips, and she drew a deep breath before whispering, "Ἐν οἶδα ὅτι ουδὲν οἶδα."

Like a punch to the gut, her words knocked the air from his lungs. It was as though she had whispered a secret password, one that identified her as a kindred soul, and Charles knew that he could not stand back and allow her to disappear from his life. He knew he ought not to address her. However, the need to reveal himself to her was stronger than anything he had ever experienced, so he opened his mouth and answered her unintentional call, "I know one thing that I know nothing."

Instantly, her shoulders tensed, and she spun around, round emerald eyes staring up into his.

Cursing himself, Charles smiled at her reassuringly, hoping that he had not just destroyed any chance of gaining her favour. "I have never before met a woman who could quote Socrates—and in Ancient Greek, too," he said, trying to express the emotions that raged through his heart.

Here, before him, was a like-minded soul, and he desperately wished to speak to her, hear her opinions and learn her thoughts with regard to the many questions that remained still unanswered despite the many secrets already uncovered.

And while his mind marvelled at the wonderful coincidence that had brought them both here this day, his heart whispered that the soft glow in her dark green eyes was unlike any other he had ever seen.

A gentle flush rose to her cheeks, and for a moment, she bowed her head. "It is my father's favourite saying," she replied, meeting his eyes once again, and he saw in her own the same surprise he felt in his heart. "He feels the lack of knowledge is its own greatest asset as it motivates us to understand what we do not know."

Delighted with the depth of their conversation, Charles nodded his head. "I suppose few people would consider lack of knowledge a desirable state." Meeting her eyes, he smiled. "However, I do see the wisdom in your father's words. He, himself, must be a man of great knowledge to have come to that conclusion."

A soft chuckle escaped her rosy lips, and the sound echoed through his heart with such tenderness that Charles had to draw a deep breath to steady himself. "I do believe so," she replied, deep affection ringing in her voice. "However, my father would not agree with your judgement of him."

Remembering his own father's thoughts that everything learnt could always be surpassed, that around the next corner waited another mind ready to challenge what he thought he knew to be true and possible, Charles nodded. "He would not? Would you say it is modesty which keeps him from admitting to the wisdom he possesses? Or rather the desire to lower the expectations of others?"

Another soft smile curled up the corners of her mouth. "While my father claims that he does not know nearly enough to be called wise, in my opinion, he is merely afraid to disappoint, yes."

Returning her smile, Charles said, "I suppose only truly wise men will ever refute any such claim. They know that wisdom is nothing to be truly gained and thus possessed for it is a futile state, always subject to change."

A gentle frown came to her face, and for a moment she seemed unsure whether or not to express what was on her mind. When she finally spoke, Charles' heart skipped a beat. "Would you restrict such a statement to men alone?"

Seeing the serious expression in her eyes, Charles understood the struggles she had faced in being recognised for the beautiful and frankly capable mind she possessed. "Not at all," he assured her. "Forgive me for my poor choice of words. Wisdom and knowledge do not differentiate between men and women; they see them as equals."

A radiant smile came to her face, and Charles suddenly felt the desire to cup his hand to her soft cheek. "Would you consider knowledge to be the same as wisdom?" she enquired next, and Charles felt as though he was being weighed.

"Not at all," he assured her once more, glad to see relief flash over her face. "Many people possess knowledge without the wisdom to understand and use it properly. Wisdom, however, exists away from knowledge and is far more difficult to acquire than knowledge."

"I do agree," she said, and her eyes shone with pure, unadulterated joy, the same joy that pulsed through his own veins. "I suppose wisdom is gained through deep reflection and careful consideration and by learning from others." Her eyes shifted to the Rosetta Stone, and a rueful smile curled up her lips.

"I assume you come here frequently," Charles observed, and she turned back to look at him, "for you seem quite familiar with this artefact."

She nodded eagerly. "I am. My father spent years of his life studying it, believing it to be the key to understanding Egyptian hieroglyphs. When he first heard of its discovery, he wept with joy for it was the day I was born, and he believed it to be a sign from the heavens." She smiled up at him, and her eyes met his openly. "I am named for this stone."

"Rose," Charles whispered, staring at her in awe before she nodded her head, a shy smile illuminating her beautiful face. Clearing his throat, Charles said, "It is a beautiful name, indeed."

Suddenly remembering his manners, he stepped forward and inclined his head to her. "I apologise. I should have introduced myself earlier." Deep down, he knew that he should never have spoken to her; however, he could not bring himself to regret his actions. "Robert Dashwood, at your service." Relieved to hear himself give his brother's name, Charles smiled at her.

The eyes that looked into his suddenly changed. The soft twinkle that he had seen there only a moment ago disappeared as her mouth opened, and she mumbled, "Robert Dashwood. You are…?"

Swallowing, she stepped back, her features hardening as she glared at him with what could only be described as hatred and disgust mixed into an emotion so deep and so absolute that it froze the blood in his veins.

The smile slid off his face then, and he stared back at her, desperately hoping that it had all been a mirage, that somehow his eyes had deceived him.

However, they had not.

"Is something wrong?" Charles asked as he helplessly watched the connection between them dissolve as though it had never existed; worse even for instead of indifference, he found himself fixed with a hateful glare, an abyss impossible to bridge.

All colour left her face, and the beautiful curl of her full lips thinned into a tight line. "I need to leave," she snapped, rushing past him.

Spinning around, Charles stared after her as she hastened toward the large staircase. His soul screamed at him to stop her; however, deep down, he knew that there was nothing in his power that could persuade her to stay.

As her footsteps echoed through the high-ceilinged room, Charles felt his spirits sink even lower than the day he had realised how isolated he suddenly was, even in a large city as London. Meeting her here today by chance, had been the ray of sunshine fighting its way through a dark overcast sky, touching the earth in but a single spot, allowing the dying flower to bloom again.

Sighing, Charles closed his eyes. What had changed? Why had she run from him? His name. He realised. She had only run from him after he had given her his name. No, not his name, but his brother's name. Had she known Robert? What reason could she possibly have to despise him the way she clearly did?

Well-aware of his brother's scandalous reputation, Charles groaned. Although he had never asked Robert for details, Charles had always allowed himself to believe that his brother would never take advantage of a young girl as sweet and innocent as Rose.

But what if he had been wrong?

4

THE GOOD & THE BAD

That night, still shaking from her encounter at the museum, Rose sank onto the settee in the drawing room of her father's townhouse, clumsily ripping the gloves off her hands.

So many emotions coursed through her heart that Rose hardly knew how she felt.

One moment, her hands froze in shock, her mind too stunned to process what had happened. Then her small frame trembled when anger seized her, anger about having been duped into feeling for the man who had ruined her cousin's life. After all, was it not her familial obligation to despise him? Did her own common sense not advise her to keep her distance lest she fall prey to his charms as well?

And yet, despite knowing all that, excited chills rushed up and down her body when she remembered the way his eyes had gazed into hers. Warm and soft, they had made her feel safe, safe to express herself without restraint, and his reaction to her mind's ideas had been so welcoming that Rose even now longed for his presence.

These delicious tingles, however, were quickly replaced by a sense of guilt when Diana's face floated into her mind.

Rose groaned, disgusted with herself. How could she feel for a man who was without a doubt lacking character?

Nevertheless, Rose did have doubts. Despite everything that she knew, her heart had seen a different man. A generous and kind man. A man who would listen and not judge her by the fact that she was a woman but only by the thoughts she expressed. A man who had treated her as an equal.

However, he had to be amiable, did he not? If he were not, young girls would hardly allow themselves to be misled by his charms. Young girls like Diana, Rose thought, and for the first time she could understand how one could make a choice one knew not to be wise.

Closing her eyes, Rose shook her head, unable to believe the situation she suddenly found herself in.

What situation? Her mind whispered, and Rose realised that although their encounter had rattled her, it had been a chance meeting after all. What were the odds of them meeting again?

Relief flooded her heart that the decision had been taken out of her hands, and yet, a hint of regret pulsed through her veins at the thought of never seeing him again.

"Are you all right, my dear?"

Flinching at the sound of her father's voice, Rose closed her eyes and took a deep breath, her hands clenched to her chest as though trying to calm her hammering heart. "You startled me, Father."

"I apologise, my dear," her father said, his eyes searching her face as he came to sit beside her. "Are you ill? You look pale." When she remained silent, he sighed. "Neither did you speak a word to me as we walked home from the museum. What bothers you?"

Rose swallowed. What was she to tell him? "I…No, I am fine. Do not worry, Father."

His eyes narrowed before he reached for her clenched hands, gently pulling them away and wrapping them in his own. "Speak to me, Rose. I can see the lie on your face."

Sighing, Rose bent her head. "I am sorry, Father. But I am not sure I can without breaking a promise." How could she explain what had happened at the museum without involving Diana?

Her father nodded. "I see." For a moment, he simply looked at her, his sharp eyes gliding over her face like those of a falcon hunting its prey. "Do I need to be concerned for you? For your well-being?"

Meeting his gaze openly, Rose shook her head, and he relaxed visibly.

"Well then, can you not tell me the essence of your troubles without betraying someone's trust?" he asked, and a curl came to his lips. "After all, you are an intelligent woman, my dear."

Smiling, Rose sighed, searching her mind for a way to confide in her father. "I believe what has me so rattled is that I am at odds about someone's character."

When she hesitated, her father nodded. "Do go on."

"From what I was told the…person in question ought to be of bad character. However, my own observations cannot confirm that." Lifting her eyes to her father's, Rose shrugged her shoulders. "What am I to believe? I am afraid I was misled."

"Misled by whom? The person in question? Or the one who gave you the report?"

Rose shrugged. "It has to be one or the other, does it not? For both accounts are mutually exclusive."

"Not necessarily," her father said, and Rose frowned. "Listen, my dear, to truly know someone takes time. Mostly, what we believe to know about someone are merely glimpses of their true selves. We all have good and bad in us; therefore, it is not easy to determine whether we *are* good or bad." He smiled at her, gently squeezing her hands. "The question you need to ask is how well you know the person in question compared to how well the one who gave you the report does? And keep in mind that quite possibly neither one of you is truly in a position to judge that person's character." He grinned at her. "Maybe what you need is more data."

Laughing, Rose looked into his twinkling eyes. "Father, you are truly impossible. However, your suggestion does have merit."

"Thank you, my dear." Rising from the settee, he brushed down his overcoat. "It is always nice for an old man to hear that his ideas are still appreciated by the young," he mumbled, heading for the door.

Rose chuckled, "If your intention is to elicit a compliment from me, Father, then I'm afraid I must disappoint you."

Turning his head, he looked at her, a smirk on his face. "You cannot blame an old man for trying."

"I do not," Rose told him with a smile. "However, I refuse to spend my days assuring you that you are not old."

"I know, I know." Opening the door, he stepped outside. "The young always have better things to do."

Sighing, Rose shook her head at him.

Downing a glass of brandy, Charles stared out the window at the carriages and pedestrians slowly making their way up and down the street. What were their troubles? He wondered. Were their lives as complicated as his?

This day had started out so promising, and when he had happened upon Rose in the museum, Charles had honestly felt as though somehow everything would fall into place as though he still had a place in this world. And now, here he was, drowning his sorrow in the early afternoon.

Again and again, his mind dragged him back to the moment, Rose's soft eyes had gone hard, the moment the smile had died on her lips and she had glared at him with well-founded hatred.

His insides twisted painfully at the memory, and a chill ran up and down his spine, making his skin crawl.

Shaking himself, Charles gritted his teeth, then set down the glass with a loud *thud* and began pacing the length of his study while his hands raked through his hair.

Cursing under his breath, he marvelled at the effect such a rather insignificant occurrence should have on his peace of mind. Why did it bother him that she had regarded him with such disgust? Granted, no one enjoyed being the object of another's aversion; however, she was nothing to him, so why should it plague him so? After all, they had only met for a brief moment that morning.

I know one thing, that I know nothing. His own words echoed in his ears, and exhausted, Charles sank into his desk chair, wondering what he didn't know.

Had Rose known his brother? The very question had pushed to the surface the moment she had walked out on him. However, a part of him had not been ready to face it, afraid of the answer he might receive.

He, himself, had never met Rose; Charles was certain of it. So her hatred could not stem from anything he had done.

But what about Robert?

Given his reputation, was there a chance he and Rose had crossed paths at some earlier point in a less than honourable manner? Had he treated her poorly? Was that why she hated him?

His jaw clenched, Charles swallowed as his mind conjured an image of his brother's hungry mouth devouring Rose's soft lips.

A growl rose from his throat, and he shook his head. Pushing himself off the chair, he once again took to pacing, the muscles in his arm flexed, his hands curling into fists.

As his fingernails dug into his palms, Charles stopped, closed his eyes and took a deep breath. He needed to think this through rationally; anything less would not bring him the answers that he sought.

Replaying the moment in the museum before his eyes, Charles reminded himself that the change in her attitude had only occurred after she had learnt his name.

Caught up in his raging emotions, he had not even noticed that at the time. Could it be that she had never even met his brother? That she only knew his reputation?

Charles frowned as doubts crept into his mind. Although her reaction to his brother's name would suggest that they had never met, the rather drastic change in her attitude indicated a personal involvement. Had it only been Robert's reputation, she would have excused herself, possibly shown signs of nervous agitation; however, would she have run from him the way she had, with hatred burning in her eyes?

Whatever the answer, he needed to know.

Sitting down at his desk, Charles took out quill and paper and began drawing up a letter to his brother; after all, he was the only one who could shed light on these muddled circumstances.

Quill in hand, Charles took a deep breath and tried to organise his thoughts. If only Robert hadn't gone off! If only he had stayed in London!

Cursing under his breath, Charles tried to calm down. He would need to be patient. Who knew when his brother would receive his letter?

Putting quill to paper, he wrote:

Dear Brother,

Apologise my bluntness, however, something has occurred that requires your immediate attention. Today, at the British Museum, I met a young woman. After we talked animatedly about the Rosetta Stone, I introduced myself, and she reacted in a rather alarming fashion.

Since she did not recognise my face, I can only assume that my name was the cause of her alarm. On the other hand, she reacted to such an extent that I have to assume a personal relationship.

Charles' insides twisted, and he couldn't help but realise how much the possibility of an intimate relationship between Rose and his brother bothered him.

Her name is Rose; I was unable to ascertain her surname.
I hope to hear from you concerning this matter post-haste!

With affection,

Your Brother

Sighing, Charles folded the letter, sealed it and rang for his butler, whom he instructed to find his personal courier and provide him with the letter. Although the man's fee was steep, he had been able to hunt down Robert before, and this time, he, at the very least, had a vague idea of his brother's whereabouts.

If only there was a way to contact him faster!

Sinking back into his chair, Charles buried his face in his hands.

The intensity with which he reacted to the events of that morning confused him. After all, Rose was nothing but a chance acquaintance. However, if she suspected anything with regard to their identity switch, they ought to be concerned.

Did she? Charles wondered. She had not given any indication that she might believe him to be…well, himself. On the contrary!

Leaning back in his chair, Charles closed his eyes and drew in a deep breath. Was his concern truly due to the potential threat to their secret? Or had the fact that the blood boiled in his veins nothing to do with it?

Why had she not recognised him before? Charles asked himself. Admittedly, his brother had looked somewhat differently before he had returned to London for Charles' wedding. The long hair. The unshaven face. The casual clothing.

However, was that enough to disguise someone? Could Rose have met his brother before without recognising him, Charles, now?

If only there was a way to know. However, there was not. At least, not now.

All he could do was wait.

5

TIES OF THE PAST

A fortnight later, Charles found himself in another ballroom full of people who eyed him with a mixture of curiosity and distrust. Pretending not to see their prying eyes, Charles ventured from room to room, seeking a distraction, however, unable to find one as his mind was still occupied with only one thing: Rose.

Ever since that day at the museum, he had not seen her again, which was not surprising at all, and Charles berated himself for his foolish hopes. He was a grown man for goodness' sakes! How could a few minutes spent in a woman's company unravel him so?

Taking a deep breath, he forced Rose from his thoughts, procured himself a drink and set his mind to idle chit-chat.

Although far from in the mood, Charles forced himself to greet acquaintances and friends even if they appeared unwilling to renew the connection and shared a few words here and there. If he was to ever walk among these people again, he would need to regain his position in their midst.

Unexpectedly, the evening progressed in a rather pleasant manner that helped Charles realise that his endeavour was not as futile as he had feared. Although surprised with his manners, most people appeared willing to converse with him as their curiosity persuaded them to turn over a new leaf.

When he returned to the refreshment table, Lady Dunston, a woman maybe a few years his senior, approached him. Her azure dress accented her golden hair, and her eyes shone like diamonds as they looked into his. Reaching for a glass, her gloved hand brushed against his not quite as though by accident.

Unsettled by her frankness, Charles cleared his throat.

"It is good to see you again, Lord Norwood," she said as her eyes swept over him in a familiar and rather intimate fashion.

"The pleasure is mine," Charles replied, courteously inclining his head to her.

An amused smile drew up the corners of her lips before she stepped closer and whispered, "The pleasure could be yours again."

Drawing in a sharp breath, Charles met her eyes, reminding himself that she thought him to be his brother, a man she had had an affair with before he had left England almost three years ago.

After they had decided to switch their identities, the brothers had spent days familiarising each other with the life the other had led. In Robert's case, that had included quite a few affairs among the English high society.

Knowing that Lady Dunston was only one of them, Charles sighed, wondering how to best extract himself from this situation without neither causing a scene nor giving her reason to suspect anything.

Fortunately, he was saved from having to think of something when approaching footsteps echoed from behind him, and Mr. Lawson joined their intimate exchange.

"Lady Dunston. Lord Norwood," he greeted them. "I hope I am not interrupting."

"Not at all," Charles assured him rather eagerly, which earned him a confused look from Lady Dunston. Ignoring her, Charles turned to Mr. Lawson. "I was hoping to see you tonight, for I believe we did not finish our conversation last time."

"We did not?"

"I believe you were telling me about your research," Charles reminded him, omitting that Mr. Lawson had had no intention of elaborating on said subject for he believed Charles or rather Robert to be indifferent in these matters.

"I was?" he mumbled, his brows drawn in concentration before he laughed and shook his head. "Let no one ever say that it is the old who are wise. For one cannot be wise when one does not remember."

Smiling at Mr. Lawson's good humour, Charles said, "In my belief, it is knowledge that can be lost. Wisdom, however, is an innate ability to understand."

Raising his brows, Mr. Lawson smirked at him. "Wise words for someone so young." They both laughed while Lady Dunston looked utterly bored. "What I do remember, however," Mr. Lawson said, "is that I promised to introduce you to my daughter."

"Certainly," Charles agreed. Although the thought of meeting the man's daughter did not appeal to him—for there was only one woman who currently occupied his mind—he welcomed the chance at escaping Lady Dunston's clutches.

"If you'd excuse us, my lady," Charles said, to which Lady Dunston generously inclined her head. Her eyes, however, showed her displeasure at being robbed of her chance to renew their acquaintance.

Following Mr. Lawson toward a small group of young ladies, Charles felt immensely grateful to the man. However, he would need to find a way to set Lady Dunston—and possibly others—straight about the nature of their *current* relationship.

As they neared the small circle of young ladies, Charles noticed their eyes travelling to him. While most of those looking in their direction eyed him with curiosity, here and there accompanied by a nervous giggle, one, however, openly stared at him, her eyes as round as plates and her mouth hanging open as though in shock.

For a moment, Charles feared that he was faced with yet another problem of his brother's past. However, when one lady with familiar golden-red hair, who had stood with her back to him, turned around and met his eyes, all thoughts left his mind, and he stared at her in awe and wonderment.

She, however, regarded him with the same loathing disgust he had seen on her face a fortnight ago.

"Excuse my intrusion," Mr. Lawson said smiling at the young ladies, "but allow me to introduce Lord Norwood."

While most of the young ladies bowed their heads and mumbled 'my lord,' Charles swallowed, forcing his gaze from the furious glow in

Rose's eyes. "It is a pleasure," he mumbled in return, feeling like a complete fool.

"May I introduce my daughter," Mr. Lawson began, holding out his hand, which his daughter took—although with a hint of reluctance. "Miss Rose Lawson."

Stepping forward at her father's words, Rose eyed him with disgust as though he was a bug she wished to squash under her shoe.

Occasionally her eyes would travel to the side, glancing at the girl standing behind her, until her father cleared his throat. "Where are my manners?" he mumbled as though to himself. "This," he gestured to the young lady who had stared at Charles before, "is my niece, Mrs. Diana Reignold."

Once again mumbling a greeting, Charles barely looked at the girl but found his gaze drawn to her furious cousin.

"I am pleased to make your acquaintance," he said, trying to shake the sense of doom that had settled on him the second Rose's eyes had come to rest on his.

Her lips pressed into a tight line, Rose raised her chin. "It is indeed," she replied, the tone of her voice, however, betrayed her true feelings.

Fuming, Rose barely managed to maintain her composure.

Out of the corner of her eye, she saw Diana's ash-white face and the tremble that shook her hands as she stared at the man who had ruined her life and now acted as though they had never even met.

"Are you all right, my dear?" her father asked, brows drawn down in concern.

Clearing her throat, Rose forced a smile on her face. "Of course, I am, Father." From the slight crinkle on the ridge of his nose, Rose could tell though that he was not convinced.

"May I ask for this dance?"

Rose's head snapped around, and for a second, she stared at Lord Norwood open-mouthed.

"What a wonderful idea!" her father beamed as his eyes drifted back and forth between them, a strange gleam in them that Rose had never seen before.

Forcing the smile back on her face, Rose turned back to the man before her.

Although his posture betrayed a hint of apprehension as though her answer could determine the course of his life, his strong jaw was set, and he looked at her with determination shining in his eyes.

Swallowing, Rose glanced at her father's encouraging face and reluctantly accepted.

When Lord Norwood held out his hand to her, she took a deep breath before slipping her own into his, relieved that their gloves prevented any direct contact.

Following him onto the dance floor, Rose felt her heart beating in her chest. Only too well did she remember her father's words! Yes, she ought to be open-minded and try to determine Lord Norwood's character for herself. However, one glance at Diana's miserable face had her pulse hammering in her veins; and yet, the feel of his touch—despite their gloves—sent a shiver down her back that made her catch her breath.

Never before in her life had Rose felt torn in such a way.

As her mind focused on the rhythm of the music and the steps that carried her around the room, Rose tried to distance herself from the man who caused her heart such turmoil. Nevertheless, whenever the dance would lead them together again and his hand touched hers, a shiver ran from his hand into hers, down her arm and through her whole body, making her quiver. Who was this man? She marvelled. Why did he have such power over her?

"You despise me, do you not?"

Meeting his eyes, Rose swallowed.

Despite the firm set of his jaw and the hardness that rested in his eyes, his voice sounded gentle, not like a challenge or an accusation.

When the dance drew them apart once more, Rose's eyes followed him, and he returned her gaze with the same frankness that rested in her own. Despite the distance, it was as though a conversation passed between them, a conversation that set the groundwork for all future communications.

Rose nodded in answer. She would be frank as would he. But would he also be honest?

"I do, yes."

He swallowed, and a hint of sadness came to his eyes. "May I ask why?"

Shaking her head, Rose snorted.

"The other day when we met at the museum," he began, and her heart softened at the memory he conjured, "your eyes held something else." Stepping close for but a moment, he whispered in her ear, "I thought you'd recognised me."

Again, a shiver went down her back as his warm breath tickled her skin. Swallowing, Rose met his eyes as the dance drew them apart once more. Recognised him? In what way? She had thought him to be a kindred soul, someone she could speak to about the things that mattered to her, someone who would answer her honestly and with the same depth that she craved after in her life.

When the music ended and they bowed to each other, Rose felt as confused as she had before. This man before her was an enigma, and she didn't know what to make of him. Her mind told her to be careful while her heart urged her to throw caution to the wind.

Rose swallowed. At one time, Diana had probably felt the same way about him. Only she had acted upon her heart's desire…and paid for it dearly.

As her thoughts returned to her cousin's cruel fate, Rose forced her eyes from the man who stood but an arm's length before her, thus, breaking the spell that had settled upon her.

Spotting Diana at the back of the room, her face still as pale as a sheet, Rose felt a deep ache come to her heart, and without another word, she turned and hurried toward her.

When their eyes met though, Diana fled the ballroom.

Guilt washed over her, and Rose hastened her step, following her cousin down the corridor, and finally caught up with her near the front hall. "Diana, wait!"

Spinning around, Diana stared at her through reddened eyes, her cheeks tear-stained and flushed. "How could you?" she sobbed. "How could you dance with him?"

Asking herself that very question, Rose swallowed before she gently took Diana by the arm and guided her through a large door that opened into the library. Fortunately, it lay deserted.

Closing the door behind them, Rose turned to her cousin. "I am so sorry. I did not mean to dance with him. However, my father-"

"You could have said no!"

"I should have," Rose admitted. "However, my father would have demanded an explanation, and I could not give him one without betraying your secret."

Sniffling, Diana sank onto the settee behind her. "He does not love me anymore."

Did he ever? Rose wondered, sitting down beside her cousin.

"He barely even looked at me," Diana sobbed, fresh tears running down her cheeks. "I thought that at the very least he would…he would…"

Closing her eyes for a moment, Rose shook her head, realising that despite everything that had happened, her cousin had still believed that Lord Norwood cared for her and had hoped for a sign of his feelings. Did love truly addle one's mind in such a fashion?

"You need to forget about him," Rose spoke, her voice soft, her words, however, vehement. "Whether he ever truly loved you or not, your future does not lie with him."

Did her own? An obnoxious voice whispered, and a shiver went through Rose at the thought of that man. She barely knew him, and yet, from the start, her heart had opened to him. Despite everything she had learnt about his character, she still couldn't bring herself to shut him out of her heart completely.

Although she knew she ought to.

"I know that," Diana whispered, twisting her handkerchief in her hands. Then she lifted her eyes and met Rose's gaze. "But I'm not sure if I can." She swallowed, and her features grew hard. "Even if he does not care for me anymore, every time I look at him, every time I hear his name, I am reminded of what he did to me. He ruined my life! How am I to forget this?"

Rose sighed. "You don't need to forget, but maybe you should forgive him and move on."

Diana's eyes went wide, and she stared at Rose in disbelief. "Forgive him?" she shrieked as red blotches crawled up her heated cheeks. "He ruined me. Because of him, I had to marry an old man and bore a child with the same dull face. A child I cannot love because every time I look at him, I am reminded of the worst night of my life." She took a deep breath and glared at Rose through narrowed eyes. "Tell me how I am to forgive that!"

Meeting her cousin's outraged gaze, Rose felt her own muscles tense. For over a year now, she had put up with Diana's moods. She had comforted her, soothed her pain and held her hand, always a kind and encouraging word on her lips.

Nevertheless, looking at her cousin now, Rose realised that none of it had mattered. None of it had made a difference. Diana was as bitter as she had been a year ago, and if she continued on this path, she would probably die a bitter, old lady, who had led a wasted life.

"He may have ruined you," Rose said, feeling a sudden cold engulf her heart, "but you let him." Diana's eyes snapped open. "Yes, he is at fault for what happened that night, but so are you. It was your choice to follow him. You knew better, and yet, you chose to pursue him."

"I l-loved him," Diana stammered.

Rose took her hand. "Did *he* ever say he loved *you*?"

Taking a deep breath, her cousin swallowed. "He didn't have to. I saw it in his eyes."

"Maybe you were mistaken," Rose pointed out. "But even if you weren't, you should not have gone after him, and you know that."

"Yes, I do," Diana snapped, jumping to her feet. "Believe me, I do! But even if he didn't love me, he should have offered for my hand after ruining me. After all, he beckoned me to follow him, he kissed me and then…" Shaking her head, Diana closed her eyes. "Because he didn't, I had to marry an old man, and I will never be able to forgive him for that."

Rising to her feet, Rose came to stand before her. "Then you will never be happy." She took her cousin's hands in hers. "I know what he did was wrong. He should have married you, but he didn't, and now, it is up to you to make the best of the life you have."

Diana took a deep breath, and a single tear ran down her red cheek. Then she nodded and stepped back. "I am getting a migraine," she said, her eyes hardening, unreceptive of the counsel Rose had given. "I need to find…my husband and go home."

Then she turned and left.

Taking a deep breath, Rose tried to regain her composure. For the second time that night, contradicting emotions raged through her heart, and she hardly knew what to think. She needed to get home, and maybe after a good night's sleep, she would find a way to make sense of everything.

On her way back to the ballroom, Rose stepped around a corner and collided with none other than Lord Norwood.

Startled for but a moment, he quickly regained his composure. "I apologise," he said, extending a hand to steady her. "Are you all right?"

After catching her breath, Rose glanced up and down the corridor; they were alone. "What are you doing here?" she snapped, stepping back.

"I was concerned."

"So you came after me," she said as though to herself as fear slowly crept up her spine. Turning around, she headed for the door. "Are you intent on ruining me as well?" she asked over her shoulder, her hand reaching for the door handle. Were there no footmen about?

Before she could return to the safety of the ballroom, a hand closed around her arm, gently pulling her back.

"Ruin you?" he asked, incomprehension clouding his face as his eyes searched hers and his hands came to rest on her shoulders. "I merely meant to ensure your safety. You left by yourself and in a rather desolate state. I simply meant to ensure that you were all right."

Taking a deep breath, Rose stared up into his eyes, which were so full of honest concern that she felt her resolve waver. What was it about this man that he could so easily tear down her walls?

"I was not alone," she whispered, disgusted with her own response to his closeness. "I went after my cousin." Shifting her eyes from his, she glanced to her side where his hands still rested on her shoulders.

Following her gaze, he tensed and immediately withdrew them, seemingly unaware of the intimate way he had touched her. He swallowed and cleared his throat. "Your cousin? I apologise. I did not mean to intrude. I...I wasn't aware you had gone after someone. I didn't see her."

Rose snorted, then took a step back. "Yes, I did notice that." Her lips pressed into a thin line as she regarded him through narrowed eyes. "Don't ever speak to me again," she hissed, then turned and entered the ballroom before her wits could abandon her.

Still, out of the corner of her eye, she glimpsed the pained expression that came to his face at her words, and once again, she wondered about the man who had just now set her world aflame.

Did she truly wish never to see him again?

Rose didn't know, and that frightened her more than anything else in the world.

A MERE ACQUAINTANCE

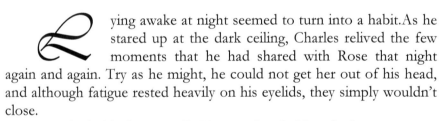

ying awake at night seemed to turn into a habit. As he stared up at the dark ceiling, Charles relived the few moments that he had shared with Rose that night again and again. Try as he might, he could not get her out of his head, and although fatigue rested heavily on his eyelids, they simply wouldn't close.

How had this happened? He wondered. How had one woman been able to unbalance him in such a way?

Closing his eyes, Charles remembered the turmoil his brother had experienced upon meeting Isabella. A bachelor at heart, Robert, too, had been swept away by a sudden onslaught of feelings, which he had not seen coming and against which he had been unable to defend himself.

Taking a deep breath, Charles wondered. Did he love Rose?

"Argh!" An agonised groan rose from his throat, and he flung back the blanket and shot from the bed. The cool floorboards under his bare feet felt refreshing somehow considering the heat that burned in his heart and shot up and down his entire body. Touching a hand to his forehead, Charles for a moment thought he was coming down with a fever.

This truly is a sickness! he thought, unable to understand how his world had turned upside down in a matter of days.

Before, he had been content, enjoying the company of friends and sharing with them his one true passion: archaeology. Whether he was at Bridgemoore or in London, Charles had always been happy with the life he had, and few things had ever been able to anger him. Never had he understood the wild emotions that so often raged within others, especially his brother. As close as they had always been, Charles had never been able to understand that aspect of his brother's character, and he had always assumed his own was more rational by nature. Had he been wrong?

Ever since that day at the British Museum, things had begun to change.

Granted, everything had started in a rather innocent way. A chance encounter had led to a friendly conversation about the meaning of knowledge. However, if he was truly honest with himself, Charles had to admit that the passion he had seen light up Rose's eyes had echoed within his own almost instantly. He had not realised it at the time, but somehow her words had touched him in a way no one else's had ever before. Not even Isabella's.

Yes, he and Isabella had shared a mutual interest in ancient cultures. However, by now, it was clear that, like Robert, Isabella was drawn to the places she had only been able to read about before. Just like his brother, she was an adventurer who wanted to explore the unknown, who wanted to see the world from a different perspective and experience everything it had to offer.

Although he could not deny that the thought intrigued him, deep down, Charles knew that he was not like them.

Charles' interests went beyond civilisations and cultures, beyond country borders and language barriers. What he craved was an understanding of human nature itself and how it reflected in the various types of people throughout time and place. A deeper meaning that connected them all, no matter their culture, language or origin.

Never before in his life had Charles met a woman who shared these desires.

Not until Rose.

Although they had only exchanged a few words, his heart and mind ached for her company, the way her wit challenged his and her thoughts completed his own.

However, if he were truly honest, he had to admit that there was another part of him that wanted her and that had never before ruled him the way they did now.

That night at the ball, he had been tempted to wrap her in his arms, to touch her and kiss her. He had barely realised that his hands had settled on her shoulders as it had seemed only natural that they should be there.

He could only hope that he had not widened the abyss that already existed between them. Was there a chance for them? Could she come to care for him?

Raking his hands through his hair, Charles paced the room. If only his brother would write back and answer the questions that burned in his heart.

From the few words Rose had spoken to him that night, he gathered that not her own personal experience had led to her revulsion of him. However, he could not be certain until he heard from his brother. Until then, doubts would remain, doubts that caused him sleepless nights, his heart thudding in his chest and his insides twisting painfully.

Whatever Robert had done to someone she cared about—possibly the cousin Rose had gone after—was there a way for him to make amends?

Staring out the window at the star-speckled night sky, Charles knew that he had to try. If he did not at least try to redeem himself and win her heart, he would regret it for the rest of his life.

And it wasn't until that very moment that Charles realised that he had already lost his own to her.

"Did you sleep well, my dear?" her father asked from behind his newspaper.

Feeling interrogated, Rose frowned, wondering if he did this on purpose in order to throw her off her guard. Somehow the lack of eye contact made her feel as though she was under a magnifying glass. "I did, yes. And yourself?"

"Quite well."

Sipping her tea, Rose waited.

"Did you enjoy yourself last night?"

A smile curled up the corners of her mouth, and she eyed her father—or rather the newspaper behind which he was still hiding—curiously. "I did, yes," she answered, intentionally not being forthcoming. Whatever her father was fishing for, she would not offer it up without knowing his reason for asking.

"Were you able to form new acquaintances?"

"Indeed, I was."

"Anyone in particular?"

Aha! As she had suspected, her father was intent on finding out how her dance with Lord Norwood had gone.

Crossing her arms, Rose leaned back in her chair. If he would only ask her directly, she might even tell him.

But what would she tell him?

For the first time in her life, Rose was keeping secrets from her father. But what was she to do? Diana had sworn her to secrecy, and she could not reveal her encounter with Lord Norwood—at least not in detail—without betraying her cousin.

Would she have otherwise told her father the whole truth? Rose wondered. After all, she couldn't quite understand that man herself and much less her own reaction to him. So, even if she had not given her word, what was she to say?

The upper right corner of the newspaper came down, and her father looked at her through narrowed eyes. "So?"

Rose drew in a deep breath. "No, no one."

Nodding, her father returned to reading his paper.

Rose sighed and reached for a muffin when a knock sounded on the door and their butler entered.

Putting down the newspaper, her father said, "What is it, Jenson?"

Rose shook her head. He was indeed doing this on purpose!

"A letter for Miss Lawson."

Lifting her eyes off her muffin, Rose watched Jenson as he rounded the table and held out a small silver platter to her, an envelope on top.

"Thank you," she mumbled and took the letter. Turning it over, her eyes went wide when she saw the seal. Although she did not recognise it, it could only belong to one person. Rose swallowed as her breath caught in her throat.

"Who is it from?" her father enquired, for once not hiding behind his newspaper. His otherwise inquisitive eyes were trained to portray merely mild curiosity as he regarded her over his steaming cup of tea.

Hesitating, Rose stared at the imprint in the red wax. Then she lifted her eyes and met her father's gaze, the hint of a smile playing on her lips. "Diana," she lied, feeling a small stab in her heart. "As I told you, she felt rather poorly toward the end of the ball last night and left early."

An annoyed expression came to her father's face. "And now she summons you to her side again?" He shook his head.

"Would you excuse me, Father?" Rose asked, knowing that she would not be able to keep the emotions that this letter would surely elicit from playing over her face.

"By all means," he said, his voice even despite the hint of suspicion that lay in his narrowed eyes.

Retreating to the drawing room, Rose sank onto the settee and for a moment simply stared at the letter in her hands. Her heart thudded in her chest, and she felt strangely reminded of Diana as though she were following in her cousin's unfortunate footsteps.

Maybe she ought to destroy the letter without even opening it. Who knew what it contained and how the words within would affect her?

With shaking hands, Rose broke the seal.

Unfolding the single sheet of paper, she took a deep breath, willing her heart to slow down. Her eyes settled on the neatly penned words, and she could not help but run her finger over the lines.

Dear Miss Lawson,

Please forgive my intrusion into your life; however, I feel the need to apologise for the distress I caused you. I implore you to believe me that it was not my intention to cause you any pain.

After a rather uneventful fortnight in London, I merely meant to reacquaint myself with the beauties of the British Museum the day we met. However, I am compelled to tell you that I was pleasantly surprised to meet a kindred soul in the very spot that has held my heart until now. Forgive me for being so frank; however I must speak my mind.

Would you allow me to call on you in order to renew our acquaintance?

Yours sincerely,

Robert Dashwood

Holding her breath, Rose stared at the words before her. Could she believe them? Or was he merely playing with her? Had her parents not happened upon them, would he have stolen Diana's virtue that night in the gardens?

That thought instantly jarred Rose awake as the tender emotions that had begun to blossom in her heart were instantly squashed by the knowledge that she could never tolerate such a behaviour in the man who vied for her hand—if indeed his intentions were honourable, which was doubtful.

Voices echoed over through the closed door, and Rose looked up just as the door opened and Diana strode into the room.

Rather shocked to see her cousin, Rose shot to her feet and the letter slipped from her hand. "Diana," she exclaimed. "What are you doing here so early?" Kneeling down, she reached for the letter as her cousin came to stand beside her.

"I came to apologise for the way I spoke to you last night," Diana said, taking off her gloves and seating herself on the settee. "I know you only meant to help me."

Quickly refolding the letter, Rose sat down beside her cousin. "Do not worry yourself," she said as her heart hammered in her chest. "I could see how distraught you were." Sliding the sheet of paper back into the envelope, Rose casually meant to deposit it on the side table when her cousin's eyes shifted to the red wax seal.

Instantly, Diana's eyes narrowed before they moved upward and met Rose's gaze. "It is from him, is it not?" she gasped, her voice feeble. "He sent you a letter."

Rose swallowed. "He did. But—"

"Why?" Diana asked, a hint of anger burning in her eyes. "Why would he send you a letter? He only danced with you once. You don't even know him."

"I don't know," Rose lied for the second time that day. "Please believe me, I did not encourage him."

For a long moment, Diana simply sat beside her, her eyes distant. "You cannot trust him," she whispered, and her eyes met Rose's. "I was foolish enough to do so and…" She took a deep breath and for a moment closed her eyes as though trying to find the strength to continue. "He will do to you what he did to me, what he has probably already done to countless gullible girls like us."

Like us.

The words echoed through Rose's mind. Never had she thought herself cut from the same cloth as Diana. They had always been so different, were to this day, and yet, they had both fallen for the same man.

"I promise I will not allow that to happen." Taking her cousin's hand into hers, Rose looked at her imploringly. "Thank you for looking after me."

The ghost of a smile flashed over Diana's face. "You're the sister I never had."

"And you are mine," Rose said, drawing her cousin into her arms.

Glancing at the letter in her hands, Rose knew that she should have burnt it without even reading it first. And although it was too late to keep that man's words from touching her heart once again, it was not too late to rid herself of the letter.

Determined, she rose from the settee and strode over to the fireplace. "To a happy future," Rose said, meeting her cousin's eyes. "For the both of us."

And with that, she dropped the letter into the flames.

Goodbye, her mind whispered, and her heart ached.

7

A CHANCE ENCOUNTER

As the days dragged on without a reply from either his brother or Rose, Charles thought he would lose his mind. Never before had his own studies failed to occupy his mind to such an extent that everything else simply faded away in comparison.

Since he was no longer considered a member of the Royal Society nor the Society of Antiquaries, Charles set out and headed to White's. Usually, he rarely spent time at the exclusive gentleman's club due to the most prominent topics discussed there: politics and gambling. However, without other options, he welcomed the chance to distance himself from the constant questions that assaulted his mind day and night.

Upon walking through the door, Charles found himself the object of quizzical looks and raised brows, which was not surprising since his brother had not been a frequent member of White's either considering that it was an all men's club.

Trying his best to blend in, Charles ventured from room to room, here and there listening in on the conversations and spending a few moments watching the Earl of Kindham beat his brother at billiards. However, Charles never lingered for a long time because neither distraction served him well as his mind continued to venture to the one woman whose determined rejection plagued him.

"I am so glad to be back in London," old Lord Tennally laughed. "Country life does not suit me at all."

Stopping, Charles glanced around the room, his eyes shifting from one gentleman to another, trying to remember their names if he knew them at all. Since they had run in different circles before, he could only conjure a handful of names. The other men, however, at least looked familiar—mostly.

"Last week's ball was quite a success. I've rarely seen so many lovely ladies in one place," another gentleman, whose youthful face suggested that he was still unmarried and searching for a wife, chimed in.

Many agreed whole-heartedly, and the ball as well as its female attendees were discussed at length. Bored, Charles only listened with half an ear, his eyes gliding over the many paintings decorating the walls when one comment suddenly had his head snap around.

"Her name is Rose Lawson. I believe this to be her first Season."

"I've never heard of her."

"Her father is the late Baron Cuthwill's second son, a real history enthusiast."

"I've heard his daughter is a lot like him."

"What a shame! She is quite beautiful."

"Why would you care about her interests? As long as she's—"

"Radcliff!" Lord Tennally rebuked the young man harshly. "Mind your manners!"

Radcliff, however, laughed, a mischievous twinkle in his eye. "All I'm saying is that considering her beauty, I do not mind her interests." Looking around the small circle of men, he raised his eyebrows. "This might be her first and only Season."

As laughter echoed through the room, Charles turned on his heels and left.

Sick to the stomach, he walked the streets of Mayfair without direction, without thought for where he was going. All he could think about was Rose.

Even though she might never accept his hand, his stomach turned upside down at the thought of her marrying a man like Radcliff.

Anger boiled in his veins, and he felt the sudden and irresistible need to strike the man down.

Stopping in his tracks, Charles drew in a deep breath, shocked at his own reaction. Never before had he experienced anything like it. What was she doing to him?

"You look troubled," a familiar voice spoke out behind him, and Charles spun around.

Coming to stand before him, Mr. Lawson's eyes narrowed as he regarded him with open curiosity. "Very troubled," he corrected himself. "I hope it is nothing serious if you don't mind an old man prying."

Somewhat taken aback and yet glad for the company, Charles sighed. "Honestly, I do not know."

"A woman then?" Mr. Lawson asked and laughed when Charles averted his gaze. "Either that or you've reached a dead end in your research."

Charles smiled. "Are you speaking from experience?"

"I am," Mr. Lawson admitted, gesturing for Charles to fall into step beside him. "I frequently feel the need to leave the house and clear my head. It helps me to focus."

"Where are you headed?"

"Nowhere in particular. I simply walk around until brilliance strikes," Mr. Lawson continued, and a grin came to his face, "or I feel too tired to walk on."

The two men continued on in silence for a few minutes before Mr. Lawson asked, "Is it my daughter?"

As though someone had punched him in the face, Charles' head snapped around and he stared at Mr. Lawson open-mouthed.

The older man chuckled, "May I take this as a confirmation?"

Charles swallowed, regarding the other man carefully before he nodded. "You may."

"May I ask what troubles you?"

"Your daughter does not care for me," Charles admitted, feeling strangely liberated at confiding in her father. "She's made her disregard for me perfectly clear."

"I see," Mr. Lawson mumbled, his eyes distant as though only half-aware of Charles's presence. Then a youthful grin spread over his face, and he slapped Charles on the shoulder good-naturedly as though they had known each other for years. "Why don't you come to supper tonight, and we'll discuss this further?"

Thunderstruck, Charles stared at him.

"Some friendly advice," Mr. Lawson whispered, leaning in conspiratorially, "others will only believe you worthy of their affections if you believe yourself to be."

Smiling, Charles nodded. Although he was far from the charmer that his brother was, Charles had never been insecure around the fair sex. However, ever since he had taken on Robert's identity, he had felt unsteady in his dealings with the rest of the world.

"Does that mean I may order another place setting tonight?" Mr. Lawson asked.

"Yes, you may," Charles said. "I'm looking forward to it. Thank you." Although he doubted that Rose would receive him with a smile, he could not bring himself to pass up the opportunity to see her again, especially considering the intimate setting.

After exchanging their calling cards, Charles headed home, his heart a million times lighter.

Turning the page, Rose sighed, realising that she could not recall details of what she had read in the last half hour as her mind was too occupied with a certain gentleman she tried her best not to think about.

Defeated, Rose closed the book and rose from the settee. Walking over to the windows that opened up to the quiet street running the length of their townhouse, Rose stared into the distance, unaware of the people walking by on the pavement.

Therefore, she did not see her father return from his walk. Noticing her standing by the window, he stopped and gave a quick wave. However, when she failed to respond, he climbed the stairs and entered the house.

Only when the door to the drawing room opened and his voice reached her ears did Rose become aware of his presence.

"You look thoughtful," her father observed, sinking into the armchair by the fireplace. Drawing a handkerchief from his pocket, he dabbed his forehead, his breath slightly quickened. "It is days like these that make me feel old," he mumbled, and Rose smiled, shaking her head at him.

"You look refreshed, Father," Rose declared, and a grin spread over her face as he met her eyes.

"Do not mock me, Child," her father chided, a humorous twinkle in his eyes. "Are you not aware that you're supposed to respect your elders?"

Re-taking her seat on the settee, Rose looked at him in bewilderment. "Of course I am. If you point one out to me, I shall be most respectful indeed."

Laughing loudly, her father shook his head as the earnest expression Rose had forced on her face cracked, and she bit her lower lip, trying to hide the smile that wouldn't be denied. "My dear Rose, you are truly one of a kind."

"Well, I suppose we are more alike than we ever thought possible." Watching the laughter lines on her father's face deepen, Rose cleared her throat. "Tell me, Father, what put you in such a great mood?"

Wiping a tear from his cheek, her father sat up and returned the handkerchief to his pocket. "My walk was quite enjoyable. In fact, I met an old acquaintance."

"You did? May I ask whom?"

Holding her gaze for a moment, her father said, "Lord Norwood."

As the remnants of a smile slid off her face, his gaze remained fixed on hers, observing her carefully.

Noticing his watchful eyes, Rose cleared her throat. "How nice."

Her father's eyes narrowed. "You dislike him."

"Well…" Rose drew a deep breath. She had feared this would happen. Despite her decision to end their connection, that man had found a way to embed himself into her life, and now, she was forced to lie to her father on an even deeper level. For how could she explain her aversion to Lord Norwood if not with the truth?

"Has he been disrespectful towards you?" her father enquired.

Rose sighed. *Not towards her. But towards Diana.* "No, he has not. However, that man has a most scandalous reputation."

Lifting his arms off his belly and settling them on the armrests of his chair, her father humphed. "Personally, I've always believed that one ought not to allow others to define one's own opinion. Frankly, I am astonished to hear you rely on rumours spread by people you have no deeper connection to."

Her father's open reproach stung, and Rose felt the strong need to defend herself. Of course, she did not base her opinion on hearsay; what she knew she knew due to a very intimate connection. However, she could never betray Diana by revealing her secret, and so she remained quiet.

"My own observations," her father continued, "lead me to believe Lord Norwood to be a forthright and truly honourable man. I welcome his quick wit and honest opinion, which is precisely why I invited him to dine with us tonight."

For a moment, Rose doubted her ears. However, when she met her father's calculating gaze, she swallowed, and her heart skipped a beat as the meaning of his words sunk to her core. "You invited him for supper? Tonight?"

"I did," her father confirmed, rising from the chair. "I thought you might enjoy some company." Smiling at her, he turned to leave. "Do not worry, my dear. For even if he does have a scandalous reputation, my presence ought to guarantee your safety." Chuckling, her father left the room.

Shaken to her core, Rose closed her eyes and, bending her head, rested her face in her hands. For a moment, she concentrated on drawing one deep breath after another into her lungs, afraid to allow her thoughts to venture to the consequences of her father's invitation.

Consequences? She wondered. Of course, Diana would learn of the invitation and be less than gracious in her reaction. However, despite her inevitable anger, Rose would be able to defend herself against her likely accusations. After all, her father had been the one to issue the invitation, not her.

Nevertheless, the more she thought about Diana, the more Rose realised that her mind merely attempted to distract her from the one thing that truly unsettled her.

Would he be able to shake her resolve? Could she spend an evening in his presence and resist his charms?

Despite feeling disgusted with herself for admitting this, Rose knew that she felt strangely drawn to him. Ever since that day at the museum, he had been in her thoughts and dreams. Not a day passed that she did not relive the dance they had shared or the feel of his hands resting on her shoulders, his deep eyes searching hers.

Even just remembering him, Rose could feel herself respond. Her heart jumped with joy, and a myriad of butterflies took flight in her belly.

Groaning, Rose shook her head, wondering about the disaster that night would bring.

8

A NIGHT TO REMEMBER

"Y ou seem less troubled," Mr. Lawson observed, offering him a glass of brandy while they waited in the drawing room for Rose. "Quite the contrary, in fact."

Charles smiled, taking a sip. "My spirits have indeed improved thanks to your kind words and even kinder invitation."

Elated at the thought of seeing Rose that night, Charles had spent the afternoon contemplating his options. Despite her open hatred of him, Mr. Lawson was kindness personified, honestly concerned about Charles' well-being. In turn, that observation had led Charles to believe that whatever had caused Rose's dislike of him, she had not shared her reasons with her father. Being ignorant of them himself, Charles could not help but wonder why.

Therefore, he was determined to further his relationship with Mr. Lawson and attempt to redeem himself in his daughter's eyes. Hopefully, she would come to see him for the man he was and not the reputation he now possessed.

For the next half hour, Charles talked to Mr. Lawson about the man's work on deciphering the Rosetta Stone until the door opened and Rose appeared.

Complementing her auburn hair, shining almost golden in the candlelight, Rose wore a dazzling gown in a deep midnight green that honoured her name, making her look like the beautiful rose she was. Or rather a brilliant Rose, Charles corrected himself as his eyes met hers, and he read in them the same curiosity and intelligence that had so bewitched him the day they had met at the museum.

As they sat down to supper, Charles was acutely aware of the woman sitting across from him. Although he mostly spoke to Mr. Lawson, his eyes often strayed to Rose, intrigued with the slight tremble that shook her small hands. Her eyes focused on the plate before her, she, on the other hand, strictly avoided looking at him, her gaze only meeting her father's before she averted them once more.

"I, myself, have not been out in society much these past few years," Mr. Lawson admitted. "I cannot say I care for it much, and frankly, there was no need before Rose came of age."

"I see." As his eyes darted across the table, Charles noticed a tinge of red colouring her cheeks. Did she mind that the topic of conversation had shifted to her? "I, too, prefer the company of like-minded friends to the deafening roar of a crowded ballroom."

Nodding, Mr. Lawson reached for his wineglass. "I hear you have spent the past few years travelling the world. What made you decide to return now?"

Sighing, Charles shrugged. "In truth, I had no intention of returning, and I probably wouldn't have if it hadn't been for my brother's wedding."

"Then we, too, are most fortunate that your brother found himself a beautiful wife," Mr. Lawson declared, raising his glass. "To the happy couple."

"To the happy couple," Charles and Rose echoed, and for a moment, their eyes met across the table.

Instantly, the breath caught in Charles's throat, and for a second, he forgot to take a sip with the others. Clearing his throat, he chuckled. "Yes, it was indeed most fortunate," again, his eyes travelled across the table, "for I cannot think of a place I'd rather be right now."

"I'm glad to hear it," Mr. Lawson said. "However, I must say that I was surprised to hear that your brother and his wife went on such an extended journey. Although we were not well-acquainted when he left, I believed him to be rather attached to his home."

Charles nodded, feeling a strange sense of detachedness at hearing himself spoken about in such a way. "He was. However, I suppose seeing each other again after two years, we both experienced a change with regard to what our hearts truly desired." Glancing at Rose, he caught her eye, and a shiver went over her. Holding his gaze for a moment, she swallowed before once more averting her eyes.

Returning his attention to Mr. Lawson, Charles rejoiced at her reaction, feeling its echo within his own heart.

"Yes, a change in perspective often helps to clear one's mind and allows one to see things more clearly," Mr. Lawson agreed before an amused chuckle escaped him. "It is as though you each took up the life of the other."

Stunned, Charles froze, his fork stopping half-way to his mouth. Then he glanced at Mr. Lawson and to his utmost relief found no suspicion in the older man's clever eyes. "Yes, it would seem so indeed," Charles agreed, his voice sounding strained to his own ears.

Looking across the table, he found Rose's eyes resting on him, her brows slightly drawn into a puzzled frown as she regarded him with interest.

Charles swallowed.

"I have to admit a part of me would very much like to see the many places from which my artefacts originated," Mr. Lawson said with a wistful smile on his face.

"As would I," Charles agreed without thinking.

Immediately, two pairs of eyes narrowed as they regarded him with surprise.

"I mean there are still so many places that I haven't seen yet," Charles hurried to explain, hoping that his voice did not shake as much as his hands did under the table. "A lifetime would not be enough to see them all."

Mr. Lawson nodded. "That is indeed true."

After supper, they returned to the drawing room, and while Charles and Mr. Lawson animatedly discussed the other's work on various artefacts, Rose sat on the settee, hardly a word leaving her lips. Few men would probably consider her behaviour strange considering that most women would not be able to participate in such a conversation. Charles, however, knew Rose's clever wit and couldn't help but wonder what went on in her mind as she watched them with rapt attention.

"Yes, I must admit that the Rosetta Stone is by far the most intriguing artefact," Mr. Lawson said, eagerness shining in his eyes. "I may not have the resources Mr. Young has, but I enjoy the insights it's granted me so far."

Charles nodded, remembering that Mr. Young was the foreign secretary of the Royal Society currently working on deciphering the Egyptian hieroglyphs that made up one third of the stone's inscriptions. "That is indeed most exciting."

"Would you care to see them?" Mr. Lawson offered before he slightly cocked his head and regarded Charles through narrowed eyes. "And please, do be honest. At present, you seem like a man very much interested in archaeology. However, from what I remember of you, I suppose I am justified to have doubts."

Charles chuckled. "I would like to see them very much. You are most kind to offer."

Nodding his head, Mr. Lawson headed towards the door. However, before he had taken more than a few steps, he turned back around. "Please, remain seated," he said to Charles, whose eyebrows rose in astonishment. "I shall retrieve my research from my study and return shortly." His eyes shifted to his daughter. "I trust that Rose will keep you good company."

Then he turned and left, closing the door behind him.

Staring at the closed door, Rose took a deep breath, confused about her father's reasons to force her into this situation; for she knew him too well to not have noticed the conspiratorial twinkle in his eyes when he had demanded Lord Norwood remain in her company. Had her father not promised that she would be safe? That his presence would dissuade Lord Norwood from doing anything untoward?

Clearing her throat, Rose focused her eyes on the pianoforte in the corner, unwilling to test her own resolve and meet Lord Norwood's eyes.

"I am surprised he is leaving us alone together."

Rose drew in a deep breath. "As am I." Then she rose from the settee and went to stand by the window, gazing out at the darkened street, which lay almost abandoned at this hour.

Behind her, Lord Norwood rose as well, and she heard his footsteps sounding on the parquet floor as he came to stand behind her. Feeling a shiver run down her back, Rose straightened her shoulders, determined not to allow his proximity to confuse her.

"I've enjoyed this evening very much," he said, his voice smooth and beckoning. "Your father is a great man. You are fortunate to have him."

Feeling her resolve waver, Rose remained quiet.

"Are you determined not to speak to me?" he asked, and a hint of disappointment rang in his voice. "Rose, please."

A shiver went down her back at the sound of her name, a shiver that made her breath catch in her throat and her knees go weak. Closing her eyes, Rose took a deep breath. "What do you want me to say?"

A relieved sigh left his lips, and he took a step closer, his breath tickling the back of her neck. "Whatever you will."

Straightening, Rose turned to face him, her hands balled into fists at her side. "It was not my idea to invite you here tonight."

"I know." Looking down at her, his eyes searched hers. "Do you mind that I came?"

"Yes." Dropping her gaze, Rose glanced past him toward the door that remained closed. Where was her father? What was taking him so long?

"That is a lie," Lord Norwood stated, and her head jerked back. "I can see it in your eyes."

Rose swallowed for she knew his words to be true, and yet, what was she to do? He was the man who had ruined her cousin's life, and he did not even have the courtesy to show remorse. "It does not matter," she said, holding his gaze. "My mind is set."

A hint of sadness in his eyes, he nodded. "I can see that, too, and yet, I cannot bring myself to abandon hope."

"Hope?"

"That one day you might accept me after all."

As anger surged through Rose, her eyes narrowed. "How dare you speak to me like this? Your reputation is widely known. Do you truly believe you can fool me?"

In answer to her words, his jaw clenched, and he swallowed, a hint of anger in his eyes. "Tell me, Rose, have I ever treated you disrespectfully?"

"I wish you would not address me so informally, my lord," she snapped, disconcerted by the loss of composure so evident in his eyes. "We hardly know each other."

He took another step closer, and his breath caressed her cheek as his eyes held hers. "It is not I who presumes to know the other," he forced out through gritted teeth. "However, you've judged me without cause."

"Without cause?" Rose's eyes snapped open, and she shook her head.

"What have I done that is so despicable to you?" he asked, his eyes drilling into hers.

Rose scoffed, "I do not know which is worse, the deed itself or that you do not even seem to recall it. Do you truly walk through life, completely ignorant of other people's feelings?"

For a moment, he remained quiet, his eyes searching hers in a rather intimate fashion that brought goose bumps to Rose's skin. Then he opened his mouth and said, "I am aware of yours."

As her hands began to tremble, her heart quickened. "Mine?"

His gaze dipped lower and touched her lips before recapturing her eyes. "Yours," he whispered as his hands gently settled on her waist.

Rose drew in a sharp breath. Unable to avert her eyes, she waited; however, he did not step closer or draw her to him. He merely stood before her, his hands resting on her waist as though they belonged there while his eyes held hers captive, daring her to accept him.

Once more, his gaze travelled down to her lips before he leaned in for a kiss. A breath's distance away, though, he stopped, his eyes darting up to her own, asking permission.

Feeling suddenly lightheaded, Rose licked her lips. She knew she ought to stop him, and yet, she could not for her heart urged her on, longing for the feel of his lips on her own.

An eternity passed before his hands came around her more firmly, and he bent his head further down toward hers. Had she nodded her head or otherwise indicated her agreement? Rose didn't know; it did not matter anyway. The only thing that mattered were the millions of butterflies surging through her middle.

When his mouth gently brushed against hers, Rose closed her eyes and abandoned all thought.

72

Her lips began to tingle with pleasure, and a fire broke out somewhere deep down, its flames surging through her body, awakening a desire firmly held in check. Reaching up, her hands curled around the hem of his jacket, pulling herself closer to him.

In answer, the hands on her back tightened before his left came up to cup the side of her face, his thumb gently stroking her cheek. Then he deepened the kiss, and his hand travelled farther back to the small of her neck to hold her even closer.

Excitement coursed through her veins, and Rose forgot everything around her until he pulled back, his lips brushing against hers once more, and whispered, "I love you, dear Rose."

As though slapped, her eyes flew open and she stared at him in shock, barely aware of the stunned expression on his face as she drew back, pushing his hands off her. Breathing heavily, Rose brushed down her dress, smoothing non-existent wrinkles. "Do not take me for a fool, my lord," she gasped, unable to meet his eyes. "I am well aware of your reputation and will not allow myself to be used in such a fashion."

When he remained quiet, Rose dared to raise her eyes off the floor and meet his.

Lips pressed into a thin line, he swallowed, his gaze regarding her with open disappointment. "If that is truly your opinion of me, I apologise for taking such liberties. I assure you my intentions were honourable." Then he formally bowed to her and offered a curt "Good night" before striding out the door.

As the world began to spin, Rose lifted a hand to steady herself against the wall. Unable to believe what had just happened, she focused her thoughts away from the turmoil in her heart and concentrated on drawing one deep breath after another into her lungs, lest she pass out.

In that moment, her father returned, a questioning look in his eyes as his gaze slid over her. "I take it our guest has left."

"Father, where have you been?" Rose demanded, anger momentarily suppressing the sorrow that began to well up in her chest. "How could you leave us alone?"

"Oh, let's not stand too much on ceremony," her father snorted, waving her concerns away. "It has been such a delightful night."

"A delightful night?" Rose echoed, her mind sluggish as though she had just been roused from a deep sleep. "Where have you been?"

"Oh, you know me," he chuckled. "I found a book on Egyptian hieroglyphs on my shelf that I forgot I had and got lost, flipping through it, trying to find the section—"

"A book? All this time, you've been in your study going through a book?"

"I guess so," her father admitted, a smirk on his face. "I suppose it was incredibly rude of me not to see our guest out, but I trust that you made my apologies." Smiling at her, he squeezed her hand, then turned to the door. "Good night, Dear."

"Good night, Father," Rose mumbled, staring after him until he had disappeared from her view.

9

A BROTHER'S RETURN

On the carriage ride back to his townhouse, Charles raked his brain, trying to think of a way to convince Rose of the sincerity of his intentions. The evening had gone so well. The way she had looked at him, her watchful eyes ever observant, trying to determine his character, had given him hope. More than once, he had felt as though she had just looked into his soul and seen him for who he truly was.

His lips tingled at the memory of their kiss. Like the fool he was, in that moment, he had believed her to have changed her mind, that somehow her feelings for him had overcome whatever atrocities his brother might have committed against her cousin. However, they had not. Had she truly believed him to seduce her in her father's house with him in the next room?

Shaking his head, Charles wondered why Mr. Lawson had left them alone. Such an action was rather uncharacteristic of a doting father.

When the carriage pulled up to the townhouse, Charles stepped out and climbed the front steps to where his butler waited. "Good evening, Milton."

"Good evening, my lord," the white-haired man whispered in his usual monotonous voice. "Your brother and his wife are awaiting your return in your study."

Charles' head snapped up. "My brother is here?"

"Yes, my lord."

Instantly, all fatigue fell from his limbs, and Charles rushed through the dark house and threw open the door to his study. Never before had he felt so relieved to see his brother home, and in that moment, Charles realised how desperately he wanted to talk to him about what had been going on in his absence.

"Little Brother," Robert greeted him, drawing him into a tight embrace. "I would love to tell you that you've never looked better," he said, then step back and eyed Charles carefully, "however, you'd know I'd be lying."

"Robert!" Standing by the armchairs in the corner, Isabella shook her head at her husband, a slightly exasperated, and yet, amused expression on her kind features.

"It's good to see you, too, Brother," Charles chuckled before he turned to Isabella. As he held open his arms, she stepped into his embrace, and the warmth that swept through him reminded Charles of how much he wished they had never left.

"We came as soon as we received your letter," she said as Robert came to stand beside her. "You look worried. Has something happened?"

Shaking his head, Charles tried to sort through the mess in his head. "No, not that I know of."

"Have you been able to find out more?" Robert asked. "What is her surname? To tell you the truth, I cannot recall a woman named Rose." A grin came to his face. "At least not one of a more intimate acquaintance."

"Robert!" Rolling her eyes, Isabella shook her head. "No wonder you have acquired such a scandalous reputation. However, I have to wonder if even half of it is true, considering that the way you express yourself would surely be enough to cast a bad light on you."

Laughing, Charles looked at his brother. Despite a more formal attire and cropped hairstyle, he still stuck out like a sore thumb. It was not only his open collar or the fact that his sleeves were rolled up, but a general air of indifference and lack of interest that hung about him.

Try as he might, Charles knew he would never be able to feign that.

"I apologise, my lady," Robert said, bowing low to his wife, a mischievous twinkle in his eyes. "I promise I will make amends later," he promised, a devilish grin on his face.

Ignoring the slight flush that came to her cheeks, Isabella turned back to Charles. "So?"

"Her name is Rose Lawson," Charles explained. "However, by now, I do not believe that she reacted to my name—or rather yours—due to a personal experience of her own but rather because of that of her cousin, a Mrs. Diana Reignold. Do you recall her?"

Squinting his eyes, Robert seemed to think hard before he finally shook his head. "I'm afraid I do not. Her name does not sound familiar, neither does Rose Lawson."

"Maybe you would remember her if you saw her," Isabella suggested, a hint of a challenge in her voice as she regarded her husband through narrowed eyes.

While Robert grinned at his wife, Charles nodded. "That's a good idea. Lord Fenton's ball is in two days. That should present a perfect opportunity for you to return to society."

Rolling his eyes, Robert moaned. "All right, dear Brother," he finally relented. "I admit we cannot ignore this possible threat to our secret. However, once it is taken care of, I swear, I will never again set foot in a ballroom full of pretentious people." Smiling at his wife, he shrugged. "Why would I? After all, I am happily married."

10

A VERSION OF THE TRUTH

*T*wo days later, hushed voices and hidden stares followed in their wake as they made their rounds at Lord Fenton's ball, which was quite understandable for it had been years since both brothers had appeared together at a societal function.

Amused, Charles watched his brother fumble for words when his old friends greeted him, speaking to him about new archaeological discoveries as well as their meaning for future application.

"No offence, Brother," Robert whispered, "but these people are mind-numbingly boring. How you have survived years of their company is beyond me!"

Not saying a word, Charles just smiled, enjoying his brother's miserable face as he and Isabella engaged in conversation about Mr. Young's work on the Rosetta Stone.

Feeling more at ease in the company of his brother and sister-in-law, Charles swallowed when Mr. Lawson escorted Rose into the ballroom. Dressed in an emerald gown, she walked as though on air, her steps graceful and light. Her eyes, however, held no sparkle, and her lips failed to smile.

Wondering about the reason for her subdued spirits, Charles pointed her out to his brother.

Squinting his eyes, Robert looked closely, his eyes sweeping over her as Charles held his breath. "I can honestly say I have never seen that woman before," came Robert's assessment after a small eternity, and a wave of relief washed over Charles.

"Are you certain?" Isabella asked.

"Of course, I am," he confirmed, wiggling his eyebrows. "I would certainly have remembered her."

With a smile on her face, Isabella elbowed him good-naturedly while Charles felt his insides twist and turn. Although he now knew that nothing had ever happened between them, the thought of Robert with his Rose turned his stomach upside down.

"Brother," Robert addressed him, "may I ask why you failed to tell us that you're in love with this woman?"

As his jaw dropped open and he stared at his brother's smiling face, Charles felt the world crashing down around him. Regaining his composure, his jaw clenched and he opened his mouth to speak.

"There is no point in arguing," his brother interjected. "It is rather obvious, which in turn makes me wonder why we are really here: to protect our secret or convince the woman you love that you are not a scandalous weasel."

Closing his eyes for a moment, Charles drew a deep breath.

A smile on her face, Isabella stepped forward, her hand coming to rest on his arm. "Why don't you introduce us?"

Charles nodded his head, then turned and headed toward Mr. Lawson and Rose. There was no point in arguing with his brother, especially not in public. First, they needed to find out what had transpired between Robert and Mrs. Diana Reignold, then he would think about his feelings for Rose.

Instantly, his heart called him a liar, reminding him that he knew perfectly well how he felt about her.

"Lord Norwood." Mr. Lawson greeted them with a surprised smile on his face. "I dare say the resemblance is uncanny."

"Allow me to re-introduce my brother, Charles Dashwood, and his wife Isabella."

While pleasantries were exchanged, Rose remained rather quiet. However, her calm eyes became suddenly lively as they darted back and forth between him and his brother. A small frown settled on her face, and Charles felt a stab of jealousy, fearing that his brother's charm had the same effect on her as it did on so many others.

"I admit I am quite surprised to see you here," Rose said, glancing at the two brothers in conversation with her father, as she and Isabella Dashwood procured themselves a glass of punch from the refreshment table. "Your brother-in-law did not mention that you were to return so soon."

"Well, he could not have told you for he did not know," Isabella admitted, a genuine smile on her kind features. "It was a rather spontaneous decision."

As her eyes returned to the two men almost identical in appearance, Rose could not help but wonder about the sense of oddity that she couldn't seem to shake. Why had Charles Dashwood and his wife returned? Had Lord Norwood asked for their assistance? Shaking her head, Rose laughed about her distrustful mind.

"He cares about you," Isabella said unexpectedly.

Surprised, Rose turned back to face Isabella, regarding her openly. "Why are you telling me this?"

A soft smile touched the woman's lips. "Because I think you care about him as well."

Averting her gaze, Rose cleared her throat as her heart hammered in her chest. "It does not matter how he feels or how…I feel, for that matter. He is not the kind of man I would ever consider."

"I see." Stepping around Rose, Isabella met her eyes. "May I ask what ruined your opinion of him?"

Staring at her, Rose shook her head. "Why do you not ask him? He is the one who can tell you what happened."

"Because I want to hear your account," Isabella said. "After all, men tend to see things differently than women."

Searching her face, Rose nodded, seeing no reason not to relate Diana's version of that night. After all, Lord Norwood could easily provide or probably already had provided his own narration, very likely painting himself the victim of a love-struck girl.

For a second, Rose wondered if Diana's account was accurate after all.

"All right," she relented, drawing Isabella away from the crowd so as to avoid anyone overhearing their conversation. "Three years ago at a ball like this one, he lured my cousin into the gardens," with some satisfaction, she watched Isabella's eyes grow round, "took his liberties with her, and then refused to marry her."

"I see." Taking a deep breath, Isabella nodded her head, her face suddenly serious, all tenderness vanished.

"My aunt and uncle hoped to avoid a scandal," Rose continued, feeling the need to explain her cousin's hopeless situation in all detail, "however, soon after that night, the rumours started-someone must have seen what happened—and from one day to the next, all her prospects vanished. The man she is married to today is not the man she would have chosen."

"I am very sorry for your cousin," Isabella said, and Rose could see her honest dismay over what she had just learnt. "However, in my heart, I know that there is more to the story than you are aware of, and so I beg of you, do not shut him out of your heart, but allow him to explain what happened."

Rather dumbfounded, Rose stared at the strained expression on Isabella's face. After everything she had heard, how could she still defend him?

11

A LATE CONFESSION

Lying awake long past midnight, Rose thought back to the rather strange occurrences at Lord Fenton's ball that night. While she had expected to find Lord Norwood among the guests, she had been thoroughly surprised to see that his brother and sister-in-law were also in attendance, and she couldn't help but wonder why.

Although Isabella's explanation of it having been a spontaneous decision was perfectly reasonable, Rose could not shake the feeling that she herself was the reason for their hasty return. Had Lord Norwood called them home? Why would he do such a thing, though?

As the night of the supper invitation rose to the forefront of her mind, Rose rolled onto her side, her lips tingling with the memory of his kiss. Remembering her own surrender to his charms, Rose felt a hot flash rise to her cheeks, and she buried her face in her hands. Never would she have thought that a man could have such power over her!

Although Rose wished she could despise him, deep down she knew that she did not. If circumstances had been different, she would have welcomed his pursuit of her whole-heartedly.

I love you, dear Rose.

His whispered words echoed in her mind, and a touched smile spread over her face. Had she been wrong to accuse him of improper intentions? Did he truly care for her?

That thought had continued to plague her until the moment Diana and her husband had entered the ballroom at Lord Fenton's townhouse.

Immediately, Lord Norwood had hastened to his brother's side, inconspicuously pointing them out. If she had not watched them so thoroughly, Rose would never have noticed how deeply the arrival of her cousin had affected the two men.

In hushed whispers, they had spoken to each other, their eyes repeatedly returning to Diana and occasionally to her, Rose, until they had become aware of her watching them.

Then they had quickly summoned their carriage and departed hastily as though time was of the essence.

Staying behind, a frown had come to Rose's face, and the rest of the evening she was barely aware of the music or the dancers around her. Absentmindedly, she had answered questions and replied to enquiries from her acquaintances.

However, she could not help but feel her father's watchful eyes resting upon her, a concerned frown drawing down his own brows.

Something was going on. Something to which she was not privy, and Rose could not shake the feeling that somehow it was important for her to know.

Lying in her bed in the dark, faces danced before her eyes, and Rose squinted her eyes, sensing that if she looked hard enough, she would see the thing that escaped her, the thing that would allow everything to fall into place.

As she pictured Lord Norwood's face, her heart began to thud in her chest and her breathing quickened. His eyes looked at her, serious, and yet, kind and honest, matching the faint smile that spoke of a passionate nature, concealed under proper manners and conduct. And yet, everything she knew about him, everything she had heard told about his scandalous endeavours, painted a different picture.

A picture that seemed to match his brother.

Although Rose had barely exchanged a word with him, it had been rather obvious that he had no interest in archaeological research. While he had nodded and smiled along to her father's explanations, the look in his eyes had spoken of sheer boredom. Contrary to his brother, Lord Norwood though had displayed rapt attention.

Rose chuckled. If she didn't know it to be impossible, she would have thought that the man she had lost her heart to—despite her best efforts to prevent it—was not Lord Norwood, but his brother Charles.

"Robert, you need to explain this!" Isabella insisted, the expression on her face strained despite her outward calm. "In my heart, I do not believe what Miss Lawson told me to be true; however, I am not so naive as to believe that you did not *earn* the reputation you have."

For once, his brother's face was serious, and Charles could see the tension in his jaw as he swallowed before reaching for his wife's hands.

After Charles had pointed out Rose's cousin Diana, his brother's reaction had been quite telling, and they had immediately returned home in order to discuss the details in private. While silence had rested heavily on their shoulders the entire carriage ride, now safely away from prying eyes and ears in his study, the truth would finally be heard.

Placing his trembling hands on the chair, Charles took a deep breath, uncertain if he was ready to hear what his brother had to say.

"What did she tell you?" Robert asked, his eyes never veering from his wife's face.

Isabella swallowed. "She said that three years ago at a ball you lured her cousin outside, compromised her and then refused to marry her."

"What?" the brothers asked in unison.

However, while Charles felt shaken to the core about this revelation, finding himself doubting his brother's character, Robert's face spoke of disbelief and even outrage.

Seeing his reaction, Charles felt his own nerves relax; this couldn't be true.

"Is that not what happened?" Isabella asked, her eyes hopeful as they searched her husband's face.

Wrapping his own hands tighter around hers, Robert held her gaze and quietly said, "No, it is not. Please allow me to explain."

Isabella nodded.

"Thank you." Relief marking his features, Robert took a deep breath.

Never in his life had Charles seen his brother so terrified of losing someone's good opinion, and a smile touched his face as he realised how much Isabella's love had changed the man Robert used to be.

"Three years ago," Robert began, "I was a different man." His eyes begged his wife to believe him. "Yes, I did have affairs—I will not deny that—but not with Diana Lawson…or Reignold. She was a young debutante, and I knew that she was…rather taken with me." For a moment, Robert actually looked embarrassed. "She would follow me around, try to engage me in conversation and have me ask her to dance." He took a deep breath. "She was eighteen, but she was…young for eighteen. Do you know what I mean?" he asked, looking from his wife to his brother. "She was not mature at all, not like Rose."

Charles nodded, understanding exactly what his brother meant for never before had a young girl caught his attention, not until Rose.

As young as she was, she was an old soul, wise in her ways.

"Then what happened?" Isabella asked, the tension slowly leaving her shoulders. "I assume you did not lure her outside."

Shaking his head, Robert closed his eyes, a rather exasperated snort leaving his lips. "No, I did not. I…," he licked his lips, "I went out into the gardens to…meet someone, but not Diana Lawson. I had no idea she followed me. I don't know why she would have. I never said a word to her."

Isabella sighed, and understanding began to shine in her eyes. "She might have thought you returned her affections. Young girls are often swept away by a romantic ideal of true love."

"Are you thinking of Adriana?" Robert asked, a soft smile on his face.

Isabella nodded. "I do not remember how often she had her heart broken after she had convinced herself that a gentleman returned her love." Sighing, Isabella shook her head. "And yet, to this day, she believes that love is waiting just around the corner. I used to think her foolish for believing so." Gazing into her husband's eyes, she smiled. "I don't anymore."

"May I ask who you were meeting in the gardens?" Charles asked, a suspicion forming in his mind.

Gritting his teeth, Robert looked at his wife, an apologetic expression on his face, before he turned to his brother. "It was Lady Dunston."

Charles nodded, remembering the lady's insistence to renew their acquaintance at a ball a few weeks ago. If she had been waiting in the gardens, she would have seen Robert and Diana together. "Then I suppose it was she who spread the rumours."

Robert nodded. "If she saw us, then, yes, she would not have kept it a secret. The only secrets she ever kept were her own."

"Then tell us what she saw," Isabella said, a hint of tension still visible in the curl of her lips.

"Of course." Robert took a deep breath. "I was waiting by the pavilion. At first, I didn't hear her, at least, not until she was standing behind me and I felt her hands run down my back." His eyes became imploring. "I thought it was she. I thought it was Lady Dunston. I would never have assumed someone else might have—"

"It is all right," Isabella said, placing her hand on his arm. "Tell us what happened."

Robert nodded. "I turned around, and I…I kissed her." He shrugged apologetically. "I suppose it took me a moment to realise it was not Lady Dunston. I stepped back, and I was quite taken aback to see Miss Lawson. Before I could explain or rather demand an explanation, her parents came upon us. Her father instantly expected me to ask for her hand, which, of course, I did not."

Closing her eyes, Isabella shook her head. "If she truly believed that you loved her, the poor girl must have been devastated when you refused to marry her."

"Possibly," Robert acknowledged. "However, what should I have done? Forgive me, but I was not about to ruin my life because some love-struck debutante thought she could manipulate me into marrying her."

"Do you truly believe that she tried to force your hand?" Charles asked. "From what I saw in her own reaction to my sudden reappearance in society as well as Rose's, she is still haunted by what happened that night, and she blames you for making a promise you didn't honour."

"I did not, though," Robert insisted.

"I believe you, Brother," Charles said. "However, that does not change anything."

"But does it matter?" Isabella asked. "Judging from Miss Lawson's reaction, you thought that she might discover that you are not who you claim to be. Considering the circumstances, however, I believe that to be unlikely. She dislikes you for treating her cousin poorly and,

86

therefore, will probably avoid any connection with you in the future." Glancing from one brother to the other, Isabella shrugged. "I do not believe her to be a danger to our secret."

"Neither do I," Charles mumbled, relieved that his brother's name was cleared, at least within their small circle.

"But that is not the problem, is it?" Robert asked, a smirk curling up the corners of his mouth as he looked at Charles. "She still thinks you a scoundrel."

"Does that bother you that much?" Isabella asked, a faint twinkle in her eyes as she turned to Charles. "Is her opinion of such importance to you? I thought you barely knew her."

Finding himself cornered, Charles looked from his brother to Isabella, knowing exactly what they wanted him to admit. His lips pressed into a thin line, he raked his hands through his hair. "Fine," he snapped as the ache in his heart grew. "I...I care for her. She is...I..."

Stepping toward him, Isabella placed her hands on his arm, a warm smile on her face. "She is the one, is she not?"

Meeting her eyes, Charles nodded.

Robert chuckled, "My little brother in love. I never thought I'd live to see that day."

Slapping her husband on the arm, Isabella shook her head. "You of all people should know how your brother feels right now. Instead of laughing about his misery, you should use that over-sized head of yours and think of a solution to this mess."

Charles shook his head, feeling defeated. "There is no solution. She will never accept me as long as she believes that I ruined her cousin's life." His eyes shifted from Isabella to his brother.

"Well, then I should think the solution is rather obvious," Robert stated, pouring himself a glass of brandy. Now that his own happiness was no longer at stake, his old cheerful self had returned. "You need to tell her the truth."

Shocked, Charles stared at his brother. "Are you insane? What if she is so furious with me for lying to her and pretending to be someone else that she reveals our secret to the rest of the world?"

"I do not believe she would do that," Robert stated, his eyes held a hint of doubt and the hands tensed around his glass.

"Are you willing to bet your future on it? As well as your wife's?" Charles asked, shaking his head. "No, I could never ask you to do that."

"Then call me selfish, but I cannot live, knowing that my happiness is built upon your misery," Robert snapped, glaring at him. "Frankly, I am a little disappointed that you would think I'd stand idly by and watch you lose the woman you love." He shook his head in disbelief. "I never would, especially not after everything you did for me."

Unsure what to say, Charles stepped toward his brother, an apologetic smile on his face. "I didn't mean to imply that—"

"Wait!" Isabella interrupted, stepping between them. "Maybe there is another way." A conspiratorial smile curling up her lips, she looked from Robert to Charles. "Do you believe she would accept you if she knew what truly happened to her cousin?"

Charles shrugged. "I have no way of knowing that. But what does it matter? I doubt that she would believe me even if I told her."

Isabella nodded. "But she will believe her cousin."

"Her cousin?" Charles echoed.

Smiling, Robert nodded. "That is a marvellous idea." Grabbing his wife, he planted a kiss on her lips, then turned to look at his brother. "I believe we need to switch identities one last time."

DECEPTION

After the longest fortnight of his life, Charles finally found himself standing in the entry hall of his townhouse, welcoming a select number of guests to celebrate Robert and Isabella's return to London.

While Isabella was dressed in a stunning, red dress that accentuated her raven hair and dark eyes, the two brothers sported the same evening attire with the exception of their tailcoats. While Robert's was black, Charles had chosen a dark navy.

Most guests were rather surprised to have received an invitation, considering that neither one of the brothers had ever truly enjoyed the role of hosting an event in the past. However, everyone invited was in attendance, unwilling to pass up the opportunity to acquire first-hand knowledge about the newly-weds' travels as well as possible gossip about London's notorious Lord Norwood.

Relieved, Charles saw not only Mr. Lawson and Rose arrive but also Mrs. Diana Reignold and her husband. A part of him wondered if the latter had been surprised to receive an invitation, considering that they had never exchanged more than a few words with Mr. Reignold the night of Lord Fenton's ball.

However, once they had arrived, Charles's outward calm stood in even greater contrast to the impatience coursing through his veins with increasing speed. His entire hopes for a future with Rose hinged on the success of this night so that as the evening dragged on Charles found himself more and more unable to focus.

All he saw was Rose.

As she entered his home on her father's arm, his heart rejoiced, not wanting her to leave these marble halls ever again. However, when she accepted Lord Radcliff's invitation to dance, he was close to strangling the man.

With his emotions wreaking havoc on his nerves, he caught his brother's eye, who grinned at him in a knowing way.

"I know how you feel," Robert said, confirming his thoughts. "However, you need to remain calm. After all, it is only a dance."

"I wonder if you'd feel the same way were it Isabella and not Rose," Charles growled through clenched teeth as he fixed his brother with an icy stare before returning his attention to the woman he loved.

His eyes thoughtful for a second, Robert nodded. "I admit you'd probably have to restrain me." Clasping a hand onto Charles's shoulder, he leaned closer. "Still, do not ruin what we have so carefully planned out," he whispered imploringly. "The dance will be over soon, and then Isabella will draw her away."

Unable to tear his eyes away from Radcliff's lecherous gaze as it slid over Rose, Charles nodded, his muscles beginning to ache with the effort it took him to keep them under his control. "For everyone's sake, I hope it'll end soon."

Robert chuckled, "I dare say, Brother, I have never seen you this way. However, I am glad that beneath your rather serious exterior rests a passionate heart after all."

"How kind of you to notice."

Robert laughed, clearly amused by that night's happenings. "In case *you* failed to notice, which I am certain you did, considering that your attention has been solely focused on Miss Lawson since the moment she stepped over the threshold," Robert whispered, "Mrs. Diana Reignold has been observing you all night."

His eyes snapping to his brother, Charles frowned. "She has?"

Robert nodded. "She tries to hide it, but let's just say, were she a spy, they would have executed her for treason by now."

Glancing around, Charles met Diana's gaze for only a second before she spun around, pretending to admire the painting above the mantle.

"Occasionally, she glances at me," Robert remarked with a chuckle. "I suppose we have her slightly confused, which I am certain will work to our advantage."

"Let us hope you're right," Charles mumbled, relieved to hear the music come to an end. As Rose bowed to Lord Radcliff, declining his request to procure a drink from the refreshment table, Charles felt the strain on his nerves fade…and for a brief moment, he thought he would faint with relief.

"There," Robert said, nodding his head toward his wife, who moved through the crowd toward Rose. "We need to go." Nudging Charles, he drew him away. "Do not worry. Everything will work out as planned."

Charles only hoped his brother was right.

"Thank you for alerting me," Rose said to Isabella as they crossed the large hall, trying their best not to seem too rushed. "Indeed, she does look a little pale."

"Do not mention it," Isabella said, her face concerned. "I noticed her looking at my brother-in-law, and after what you told me about what happened between them in the past, I am not surprised to see her so affected. It must be hard for her to see him again."

Rose nodded. "It is. Seeing him reminds her of the wrong turn her life took that night." Glancing at her cousin's wandering eyes, Rose sighed. "Is there any place she could rest?"

Isabella nodded. "The back drawing room."

As they reached Diana's side, she shrank back before a forced smile drew up the corners of her mouth. "Goodness, you startle me. I did not see you coming. I suppose I was rather…distracted."

"Come with me," Rose whispered, drawing her cousin's arm through her own.

"Where are we going?"

Seeing Diana's bewildered face, Rose smiled at her reassuringly. "Just come with me. You need to rest."

"Rest?" her cousin mumbled, her forehead in a frown. "What do you mean?"

Smiling, Rose pulled Diana through the crowd, following Isabella as she led them through an arched doorway and down a long corridor. With each step they took, the music faded and the guests voices grew dimmer.

"In here," Isabella said, holding open the door to the drawing room.

Pulling her cousin inside, Rose urged her to sit down on the settee, then hastened to pour her a glass of water. "Here, drink this. It will help calm your nerves."

Judging from the red blotches on her cheeks and neck, Diana was quite agitated. Rose could only hope that she would calm down and allow her to take her home without making a scene. Who knew what would happen if her nerves snapped and she found herself compelled to confront the man who had ruined her life?

"My nerves?" Diana asked, confusion clouding her eyes. "I do not understand."

"Then allow me to explain."

Spinning around at the sound of his voice, Rose stared at the very man responsible for her cousin's rattled state of mind.

Behind her, Diana gasped in shock.

Squaring her shoulders, Rose glared at him. "What are you doing here?" she snarled before her eyes slid sideways and came to rest on Isabella.

"I apologise for the deception," the young woman said, honest regret shining in her dark eyes. "However, there is something you need to know."

"I don't care," Rose spat, holding out her hand to her cousin. "We are leaving."

"No, you're not," Lord Norwood stated, unflinching determination visible in his eyes. Striding toward them, he looked at Diana as though assessing her character before stopping in front of Rose, his tall stature blocking their path. His eyes met hers, and what she saw there, Rose didn't understand. For a moment, she felt as though she was looking at a stranger.

"I, too, apologise for luring you here under false pretences," he conceded. "However, there—"

Rose snorted. "You are making quite the habit of it, my lord. First, you compromise my cousin and refuse to marry her, then you have the audacity to speak to me of love," his eyes widened slightly, "and now, after inviting us into your house, you refuse to let us leave?" Rose shook her head as her heart hammered in her chest. Never before had she felt so overwhelmed. Oh, if only her father were here!

He took a step toward her. "I assure you no harm will come to you." Then his gaze momentarily shifted to Diana. "However, I believe I have the right to defend myself against the accusations laid at my door or would you deny me that?"

Rose took a deep breath. Unfortunately, his request was not unreasonable. "What do you hope to accomplish by twisting the truth of that night?" she demanded. "As I understand it, it was not your only wrongdoing. You cannot possibly hope to redeem yourself in the eyes of the world."

Holding her gaze, he shook his head. "I do not," he said before taking another step closer. "I only hope to redeem myself in yours."

Taken aback, Rose drew in a deep breath. "But why?"

A soft smile came to his lips as he looked down at her with kind eyes. "I believe you know that." Nodding to her, he turned and faced Diana. "I wish to ask you a few questions, and all I ask is that you answer honestly."

Pale, Diana stared at him with wide eyes.

"Leave her alone," Rose demanded, stepping around him. "She has been through enough."

His lips thinned as he regarded her. "Then allow me to ask you something. Was your cousin's account of what happened that night the only reason you refused me?"

Rose drew in a sharp breath as all eyes turned to her. Was it? She asked herself.

"I thought so," he said, reading the answer in her eyes. Then he nodded his head at her, and once again turned to Diana. "Why did you follow me out into the gardens that night?"

Blinking, her cousin stared at him before her eyes shifted to Rose and back again. "I…" Her eyes narrowed as though in disbelief. "You are really here," she whispered, a soft smile coming to her lips.

Lord Norwood cleared his throat, then sat down on the edge of the settee, maintaining an appropriate distance, and met Diana's eyes. "Why did you follow me? Did I ask you to?"

Although Rose felt compelled to stop him and protect her cousin, her feet wouldn't move. The pulse hammered in her veins, and she found herself looking at Diana, eagerly awaiting her answer.

"No," Diana whispered, her eyes distant as though her mind was somewhere far away. "At least, not in words." She smiled at him, and the devotion shining in her eyes broke Rose's heart. "But I knew how you felt, and so I followed you. I knew if you only had the chance to speak your heart's desire, you would ask for my hand." The smile died on her face, and an incredible sadness came to her eyes. "Why didn't you?"

Lord Norwood swallowed, and Rose was surprised to see compassion on his face. "I do not mean to hurt you; however, I would be lying if I told you that I have ever desired your hand in marriage." He paused, his eyes searching Diana's face. "I never spoke to you of love. Nevertheless, I do want to apologise for the misunderstanding that night."

As her breathing quickened, Diana shook her head, tears brimming in her eyes. "But you kissed me!"

"I did," Lord Norwood admitted, and Rose drew in a sharp breath as a wave of disappointment rolled over her, "but I thought you were someone else."

Rose frowned. "How could you—?"

"Lady Dunston," Diana exclaimed unexpectedly. "She was always around you," she added, a hint of disgust in her voice as big tears rolled down her cheeks. "She told me to leave you alone. She told me that a man like you would never be interested in a *girl* like me."

An apologetic smile on his face, he looked at her. "It was not her place to speak to you like that. However, she was not wrong. I was not looking for love that night, but I knew you were. I suppose I should have made myself clear." Shrugging, he sighed. "I never thought you would come after me, and when your arms came around me from behind, I didn't know it was you. I just turned around and…"

A wistful smile came to Diana's face. "I have never been kissed like that, not before and not since."

Hearing her cousin's words, Rose felt her own lips begin to tingle as she remembered the night her father had left them alone in the drawing room.

Then, his mere presence had sent shivers up and down her body, and she had curled her fingers into fists to keep from reaching out to him.

Now, however, the man who spoke so kindly to Diana seemed different. He had the same voice, the same eyes, and yet, they did not touch her as before.

Something had changed.

13

THE MAN SHE LOVES

fter switching tailcoats with Charles, Robert had gone after his wife in order to confront Diana as himself and hopefully prove to Rose that he had not intentionally ruined her cousin.

Charles, on the other hand, had been forced to remain behind. After all, what would their guests say if they all vanished from their own party at once?

Devoting himself to entertaining his guests, Charles made his rounds, exchanging pleasantries and ensuring that everything went smoothly. However, after a half an hour, his mind felt numb and his heart burned, his feet eager to follow after his brother.

Mumbling an excuse, he set off down the corridor, the sound of his footsteps echoing off the walls. Stopping outside the door, Charles listened carefully; he could only hear hushed voices and was unable to make out what was said.

Determined, he quietly opened the door and found Diana sobbing on the settee, his brother beside her, speaking in low tones. Isabella stood by the door and a hint of surprise showed in her eyes as she saw him. However, after a moment of hesitation, she ushered him in, and the ghost of a smile on her face gave him hope.

Then, his eyes turned to Rose.

When she met his gaze, her eyes narrowed before they shifted back to his brother.

"I need to go," Diana declared as she brushed the tears from her cheeks. "I need to go." Jumping to her feet, she turned to the door, humiliation clearly visible in her eyes.

Rose hastened after her.

"No, don't." Turning to face her cousin, Diana shook her head. "I need to be alone."

"At least, allow me to escort you back to your husband," Rose suggested, reaching for her cousin's hand.

"No!" Diana shrank back, shaking her head. "I can't. I…He is the last person I want to see right now."

"The library is down the corridor to your right," Isabella said, compassion resting in her eyes. "You will find it empty."

Diana nodded. "Thank you." Then she turned and left, her footsteps echoing down the hall.

Turning back around, Charles met his brother's eyes as he rose from the settee. A strained look on his face, Robert inconspicuously shrugged his shoulders, and Charles wondered how Rose had reacted to her cousin's revelations.

Facing her, Charles was momentarily surprised when she turned away from him and walked up to his brother. Then, however, he reminded himself that at least presently she believed his brother to be him…at least the him she had met a few weeks ago.

How had life ever become this complicated? Charles asked himself, shaking his head in exhaustion.

Meeting his brother's eyes, Rose smiled, and Charles felt his insides turn upside down before she opened her mouth and said, "Εν οίδα ότι ουδέν οίδα."

While his brother stared at her with a rather dumbfounded expression on his face, Charles closed his eyes as happiness warmed his heart and a deep smile spread over his face.

Beside him, Isabella chuckled.

A deep frown on his face, Robert looked lost. "He knows…eh…I'm sorry, but my Latin has never been good to begin with." Crinkling his nose, he looked at Charles through squinted eyes.

Shaking his head at his brother, Charles stepped forward, just as Rose turned to look at him and their eyes met. "I know one thing that I know nothing," he translated, and a knowing smile lit up her beautiful features.

"It was never you, was it?" Rose asked, her watchful eyes searching his face. "You are not Lord Norwood, are you?"

"What?" Robert exclaimed, shock evident in his voice.

Smiling, Isabella held out her hands to him, and he drew her into his arms. "Women always recognise the man they love," she whispered, tilting up her head for a kiss.

At Isabella's words, Charles' gaze returned to Rose, whose cheeks burnt in a brilliant pink as she looked at him with shy eyes.

"We should return to our guests," Isabella announced, ushering her husband toward the door.

"Wait," Robert said, pulling off his tailcoat. "We need to switch back." After he had once more donned his black tailcoat and Charles had shrugged into the navy one, Isabella once more tried to pull him toward the door. However, Robert stopped, a smirk on his face, "Do you think we should leave them alone…and unchaperoned? After all, isn't that precisely what got us into trouble to begin with?"

"You do have a devilish streak," Isabella said, her eyes smiling as she finally managed to usher Robert out the door.

"Admit it," he mumbled. "That's why you love me."

The door closed behind them.

"I apologise for the deception," Charles said, his hands gesturing widely, including everything that had happened since before the day he had met Rose at the museum. "There was no other way for them to be together," he explained, feeling cautiously exhilarated by the soft smile on Rose's face as she listened patiently. "Only after Isabella and I were married did she and my brother meet. Moments after actually." Shrugging his shoulders, he sighed. "What should we have done? There was no other way."

Licking her lips, Rose nodded, her eyes thoughtful. "You gave up your life for him," she whispered before her gaze met his once again, and a soft smile came to her face. "I've always wondered what it would be like to have a brother or sister."

"Robert and I are very different," Charles said, taking a step closer. "We always have been, but we've also always been there for each other no matter what the consequences. He would have done the same for me." Her eyes rested on his, and for a second, Charles thought to see a hint of doubt in them. "He can be reckless, but he would never intentionally hurt someone. I am sorry about what happened with your cousin, but I believe my brother when he says that it was a misunderstanding."

For a moment, Rose's head sank, and Charles held his breath. Then she took a deep breath and met his gaze once more. "I believe him, too," she whispered, a slight tremble in her lips. "Diana, too, can be rash in her decisions."

A deep smile came to Charles' face at her words, and all of a sudden, he felt a million times lighter. "Do you believe me then?"

"Believe you?"

Drawing a deep breath, he took another step closer and reached for her hands.

Though hesitant at first, Rose soon relaxed, her small hands resting safely in his own.

Gazing into her eyes, Charles smiled. "That I love you," he clarified, delighted with the slight blush that came to her cheeks.

"I do, yes," she whispered, averting her eyes for only a moment. "I think I've known ever since—"

"—the day at the museum," Charles finished for her, and she smiled at him in answer. "It broke my heart when you walked away from me after learning my name."

"I'm sorry, but…"

"I know. There is nothing to apologise for." Squeezing her hands, Charles took a deep breath, his eyes held captive by the humming glow in hers. "I know I still need to speak to your father," he said, and Rose swallowed, her eyes widening, "but I need to hear your answer now or I am certain I will lose my mind."

Licking her lips, Rose smiled up at him.

"Rose Lawson," Charles said, his heart beating rapidly in his chest, "will you agree to marry me?"

Stepping closer, she raised herself on her tiptoes and planted a soft kiss on his lips. "I've been wanting to do that ever since I met you." A delighted smile came to her face before she nodded. "Yes, I will marry you."

In that moment, all doubt and misery fell from him, and Charles drew the woman he loved into his arms and swung her around in a circle, exhilarated by the sudden happiness that washed over him.

Laughing, they lay in each other's arms as the tension of the last few weeks left their bodies and their hearts grew light with hope and promise.

"I shall speak to your father immediately," Charles declared, setting her back on her feet.

Rose smiled. "I do not believe it will come as a surprise to him." Raising his eyebrows, Charles looked at her. "If he wants to be, he can be very perceptive, and I think that he realised how I felt before I was even able to admit it to myself."

"Then you think he will not deny his blessing?"

Rose shook her head. "He would never stand in the way of my happiness," she whispered, tilting up her head. "And I need you to be happy."

Smiling, Charles lowered his head to hers, delighted at the thought to have Rose by his side for the rest of his days.

Never would he have imagined that such happiness was possible.

However, it was, and he would cherish it for the rest of his life.

When the festivities had finally come to an end and all the guests had left, they all gathered in the rather snug front parlour, a glass of champagne in their hands to toast Charles' and Rose's upcoming wedding.

An arm around Rose's slender waist, Charles felt like the happiest man alive. How natural it felt to touch her! To hold her hand! Kiss her lips and draw her into his arms!

Never would he have believed that everything would turn out the way it had. Despite his hopes for a future with Rose, deep down Charles had believed that either he or his brother would have to sacrifice for the other to be happy.

However, he had never been so relieved to be proven wrong.

"To Rose and Robert," Robert toasted and raised his glass, his eyes twinkling as they moved from his wife to his brother before coming to rest on Mr. Lawson. "I wish you all the happiness in the world. May your love always be true and strong!"

"Hear! Hear!" the others echoed, their faces lit with joy, and once more, Charles drew Rose into his arms.

"This proves to be quite an astounding night," Mr. Lawson marvelled, a smirk on his face as he looked back and forth between the two brothers.

Seeing Rose's face sober, Charles swallowed, wondering what she had seen on her father's face that had eluded him.

"Two brothers reunited," Mr. Lawson continued, "and a wedding announced. To be frank, after our last encounter, I doubted that Rose would ever agree to a proposal. She seemed quite adamant in her opinion of you."

Clearing his throat, Robert chuckled. "I suppose love does conquer all."

Mr. Lawson nodded, a gleam in his eyes that sent a chill down Charles' back. "So it would seem." He turned to Robert. "Given the intimate connection between our two families, I am quite pleased to think that we shall have ample opportunity to discuss my translation of the Rosetta Stone." Robert paled. "Few people truly enjoy such discussions—with the exception of my dear Rose, of course—which makes me cherish this opportunity all the more." Clasping his hands in delight, he sighed. "We shall spend endless days discussing the meaning and importance of Egyptian hieroglyphs for our modern languages."

Robert swallowed as his eyes darted from Mr. Lawson to his wife and then to Charles as though seeking help.

"I know that dear Robert is not truly interested in these matters," Mr. Lawson continued as he nodded at Charles. "Although he has tried to participate in these discussions, I suppose it was only for Rose's sake." Mr. Lawson shook his head. "No, I shall not bother him with this any longer now that I have an equal-minded friend to share this with."

Laughing, Rose placed her hand on her father's arm. "Do not torture him, Father." Her eyes darted to Robert before returning to her father's. "Say plainly what is on your mind."

Meeting his fiancée's gaze, Charles swallowed as his suspicions were confirmed.

Chuckling, Mr. Lawson squeezed her hands. "I apologise," he said, looking at Robert. "You do look truly ill, my friend. Is the thought of archaeological discussions so troubling to you?"

Robert swallowed. "No, certainly not. I have always enjoyed…that."

"Father!" Rose called. "Please."

Sighing, Charles closed his eyes before turning to Mr. Lawson. "How long have you known?"

A mischievous smile came to the old man's face. "Oh, a while," he admitted with a chuckle.

"Known what?" Robert asked.

"That I am you, and you are me," Charles stated plainly, and his brother's eyes grew wide for the second time that night.

"Why didn't you say anything, Father?" Rose asked, shaking her head at him.

Mr. Lawson shrugged. "Quite frankly, I was having too much fun."

Everybody laughed, except for Robert, who still looked a little green around the eyes.

"Do not worry," Mr. Lawson said to him, placing a comforting hand on Robert's shoulder. "I shall not trouble you with archaeological discussions. After all, for that I have my daughter and future son-in-law."

Exhaling with relief, Robert chuckled. "To be honest, that is the best news I've received all day."

Charles laughed. "The best news, dear brother?"

Robert shrugged his shoulders apologetically. "I love you, Charles, but I won't survive another one of these so called discussions. How you do it is beyond me!"

Mr. Lawson sighed. "Oh, dear boy, it's a matter of the heart! You cannot possibly understand until yours, too, has been stolen."

A smile on his face, Robert nodded as he turned to look at Isabella, his eyes shining with love. "That, I understand."

"As do I," Charles whispered, pulling Rose into his arms yet again, enjoying the feel of her snuggling against him as she gazed up into his eyes. "As do I."

EPILOGUE

 itting beside her husband in the small chapel at Bridgemoore, Diana felt tears sting the corners of her eyes as the priest pronounced the happy couple man and wife.

Almost delirious, Rose turned to her new husband, tears of joy running down her cheeks as he embraced her, quite unwilling to let her go as a stream of well-wishers approached them. A big smile on his face, Lord Norwood accepted the congratulations of family and friends, all the while keeping his hand closed over his wife's as it rested in the crook of his arm.

They looked happy, Diana thought, and a tear rolled down her cheek. And although her heart ached in her chest, she knew that Rose deserved to be happy. After all, her cousin had always stood by her, doing her best to see her happy.

Only Diana wasn't happy. She knew she never would be. After all, the only man she had ever loved was now married to her cousin. And what hurt even more was that he had never loved her.

Notorious Norwood had finally chosen a wife, and all of London marvelled at what a special woman she was, considering that neither fortune nor connection could have promoted her to him.

Dabbing a handkerchief to her eyes, Diana glanced at her husband.

Objectively, she had had a lot more to offer than her cousin, and yet, her husband had never looked at her twice.

Twenty years her senior, he had agreed to marry her after the rumours had started only because he wished to align himself with titled families. Despite his fortune, his lack in amiable qualities as well as appeal had often hindered his pursuit of a young lady from a titled household.

Only Diana didn't have a choice. Admittedly, her own *wrong* choice had led her down that path; however, her heart still ached for the love that shone so evidently in her cousin's eyes.

What would it feel like to be loved that way? She wondered.

Sighing, Diana closed her eyes, knowing that she would never know.

She had wasted her heart on a man, who had never cared for her, and now it was too late.

Her fate was sealed.

ABOUT BREE

Amazon bestselling author, Bree Wolf has always been a language enthusiast (though not a grammarian!) and is rarely found without a book in her hand or her fingers glued to a keyboard. Trying to find her way, she has taught English as a second language, traveled abroad and worked at a translation agency as well as a law firm in Ireland. She also spent loooong years obtaining a BA in English and Education and an MA in Specialized Translation while wishing she could simply be a writer. Although there is nothing simple about being a writer, her dreams have finally come true.

"A big thanks to my fairy godmother!"

Currently, Bree has found her new home in the historical romance genre, writing Regency novels and novellas. Enjoying the mix of fact and fiction, she occasionally feels like a puppet master (or mistress? Although that sounds weird!), forcing her characters into ever-new situations that will put their strength, their beliefs, their love to the test, hoping that in the end they will triumph and get the happily-ever-after we are all looking for.

If you're an avid reader, sign up for Bree's newsletter at www.breewolf.com as she has the tendency to simply give books away. Find out about freebies, giveaways as well as occasional advance reader copies and read before the book is even on the shelves!

Connect with Me:

Follow me on Amazon:
http://www.amazon.com/Bree-Wolf/e/B00FJX27Z4

Follow me on Goodreads
https://www.goodreads.com/author/show/7333700.Bree_Wolf

Friend me on Facebook:
https://www.facebook.com/breewolf.novels

Follow me on Twitter:
https://twitter.com/breewolf_author

A Forbidden Love Novella Series

Overview

#1 The Wrong Brother

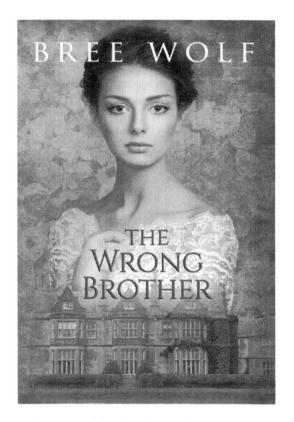

She gave him her hand in marriage.
Her heart, however, was stolen by his brother.

Despite her parents' deep love for one another, ISABELLA CARRINGTON has always favoured her mind over her heart.

Meeting CHARLES DASHWOOD, she quickly decides that he is the one for her. After all, he has all the qualities she appreciates in a man; he is kind, honest, and most of all dependable.

At least until her wedding day, when Isabella suddenly desires someone entirely different, or doesn't she?

In the very moment, Isabella whispers her 'I do', her eyes catch the glimpse of another man. A man whose eyes look unnervingly familiar, and yet stir a longing within her heart and soul she has never known.

Just as she gives her hand to Charles Dashwood, her heart is stolen by none other than her husband's notorious twin, Robert.

When mind and heart do not go hand in hand, can there be a happily ever after?

#2 A Brilliant Rose

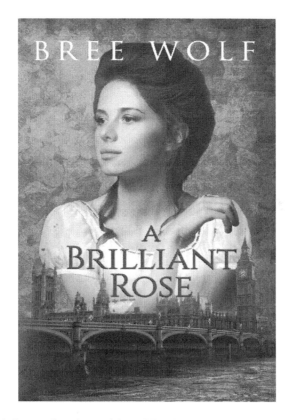

**She is obligated to hate him. Her heart, however, disagrees.
If he cannot prove himself worthy, he will lose her forever.**

When ROSE LAWSON meets a handsome, and yet, intelligent man in the British Museum, she quickly fancies herself in love. However, upon learning the man's name, anger boils within her. She has heard his name before. She knows who he is, and she knows that he is the devil incarnate.

If only her heart and mind didn't disagree so strongly, she could hate him with all the passion she possesses….and he deserves.

Torn from his old life, CHARLES DASHWOOD finds himself wandering the British Museum alone. Gone are his friends with whom he shared his interest in antiquities. Gone is their companionship.

In his desolate state, he comes upon a young lady, who seems to share the very passion he is now forced to ignore. A stimulating conversation ensues, which takes a turn for the worse when she learns his name...or rather his brother's name.

All of a sudden, Charles is faced with a problem not of his own making. From what he can gather, Rose has met him...or rather his brother...before, and unfortunately, her opinion of him could not be lower.

Will Charles be able to win Rose's heart without betraying his brother? Will his brother stand idly by and watch as Charles loses the woman he loves in order to keep his secret?

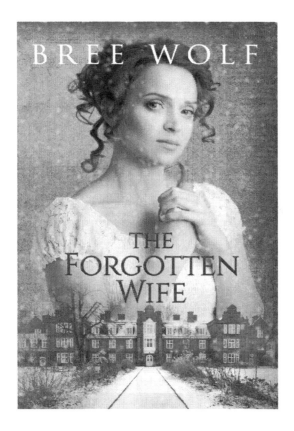

They married for love.
Now, he does not remember her.

WILLIAM EVERETT, Earl of Harrington, cannot remember the past few years of his life.

One moment of carelessness destroyed everything and tied him to a woman he does not recognise. Her sad eyes follow him wherever he goes, always hopeful, and every day, he does not remember her, the pain resting in those gentle eyes grows and grows.

Guilt claims William's heart. He knows he ought to love her. But how can he love someone he doesn't even remember?

CATHERINE EVERETT, Countess of Harrington, is devastated.

After a riding accident, her husband looks at her and sees a stranger. Gone are the years they spent together. Gone is the love that always shone in his eyes. In its place, she sees doubt and uncertainty.

Unwilling to share her life with a husband who once loved her but now only feels the ties of obligation, Catherine risks it all and agrees to her sister's daring plan.

Will Catherine find a way to reclaim her husband's heart? Or is a love once lost gone forever?

#4 An Unwelcome Proposal

He proposed. She said no.
Will she regret her answer?

All his life, WESLEY EVERETT has watched other men fall in love. Now, when he finally does find a woman who brings a flutter to his heart, she could not be less interested.

CHRISTINE DANSBY does not believe in marriage. She has a family she adores, friends who adore her, and a wardrobe that would put the queen herself to shame. What would she need a husband for? After all, life is far too exhilarating to settle down!

Will Wesley take 'no' for an answer? Or will be able to convince Christine that marriage is far from boring?

LOVE'S SECOND CHANCE SERIES

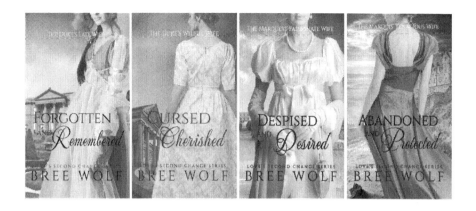

A FORBIDDEN LOVE
NOVELLA SERIES

For more information, visit

www.breewolf.com

READ AN EXCERPT OF

The Forgotten Wife

(#3 A Forbidden Love Novella Series)

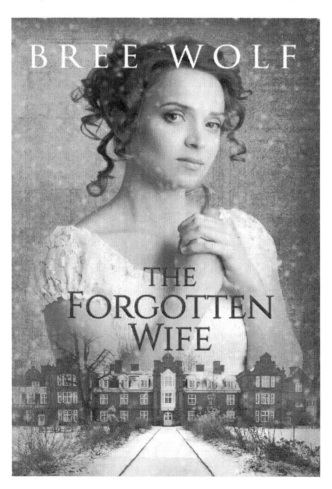

PROLOGUE

England, November 1818 (or a variation thereof)

"How did you sleep, my dear?" William Everett, Earl of Harrington, asked his wife across the breakfast table. His eyes sparkled with mischief as they held hers, and the corners of his mouth curled up into a suppressed smile before he glanced at his mother seated to his other side.

Very much aware of her mother-in-law's presence, Catherine swallowed, and her cheeks warmed as images of the previous night drifted into her mind. "Quite well," she whispered, her voice shaking. "And you?"

Her husband took a sip from his tea, his face non-chalant as though they were discussing foreign affairs. However, when he looked up and their eyes met once more, Catherine's breath caught in her throat at the vivid memories she saw there. "Extraordinarily well," he said in a voice that betrayed nothing of the emotions so evident on his face.

Smiling, Catherine shook her head at him, praying that her mother-in-law was as oblivious to their conversation as she looked.

"I, too, slept well," the dowager countess said, and Catherine flinched, "if anyone cares to know." Sipping her tea, the older woman glanced from her son to her daughter-in-law and back to her son, her eyes unreadable.

Catherine swallowed.

"That is wonderful, Mother," William said, a gentle smile on his face, before he returned his attention to the cup in his hands.

Following his example, Catherine dropped her gaze, afraid her eyes might betray what her thoughts could not abandon.

Seconds ticked by as they ate in silence, and with each, it became more and more unbearable for Catherine not to look up into her husband's face. After a small eternity, she glanced in his direction from under her eyelashes and caught him winking at her.

Unable to stop herself, Catherine chuckled.

"Is something amusing, dear?" the dowager countess asked.

"Nothing. Just a frog in my throat." Forcing her gaze from the mischief in her husband's eyes, Catherine cleared her throat and tried her best to focus her thoughts on the view before her.

More snow had fallen during the night covering Harrington Park with a thick blanket. The sun shone, and the sky sparkled in a clear blue, white clouds drifting lazily across the estate.

"I've rarely seen such beauty," Catherine marvelled at the sight before her.

"Neither have I."

As her gaze left the winter landscape outside the window, Catherine found her husband smiling at her once more, his eyes aglow as he gazed at her lovingly. Although more than a year had passed since their whirlwind romance, every day reminded her of the powerful emotions that had seized them both so abruptly.

It had been Catherine's third season, and yet, not once had she been tempted to give her heart to one of the many gentlemen she had met during that time. Unlike her older sister, Catherine had always dreamed of true love, and when her third season had proved as disappointing as the previous two, she had feared love would never find her.

But it had.

It had been the last ball of the season, and Catherine's mood had been consequently bad when out of nowhere their eyes had met across the room. Like two magnets, they had drifted toward each other, following the invisible bond that had so unexpectedly formed between them.

It had felt like destiny as William and his brother had only just returned from their grand tour on the continent. Just in time for the last ball of the season.

Lost in each other, they had danced and talked, strolled through the gardens and gazed at the stars, and by the end of the night, William had asked for her hand.

Her parents had been quite taken aback. However, after fearing that Catherine, like her sister, would come to look upon marriage as a hindrance in life, they quickly gave their consent.

"If you'll excuse me, I feel another chill coming on," the dowager countess said, her eyes looking at the cold winter day with a hint of disgust.

"Of course, Mother."

Rising from her chair, the dowager countess strode from the room, a slight tremble in her hands.

"Do you think we should call for Dr. Martin?" Catherine asked.

William chuckled. "I do not believe that she's ill. She merely hates the cold. It's always been like this." He reached out a hand and gently placed it upon hers. "Do not worry. She'll be fine."

Catherine nodded. "So? Is your brother coming today?"

"He should be here soon. We'll go for a ride down by the lake." A deep smile came to her husband's face. "It's been a long time."

Squeezing his hand, Catherine smiled. "I know what you mean. Only being one year apart, my sister and I have always been inseparable." She sighed. "A lot has changed during the last year."

Grinning, William met her eyes. "Do you regret marrying me?"

Catherine laughed. "Not for a moment," she assured him. "Not for a moment."

A deep smile came to his face, and rising from his chair, he pulled her into his arms. "Neither do I," he whispered before his lips gently brushed over hers.

Leaning into him, Catherine enjoyed the gentle shivers that danced down her back. "You're impossible," she whispered.

William smiled. "And you're impossible to resist." His words fell against her lips as he answered her silent question the way he always did.

Yes, he loved her.

Wrapping her arms around his neck, Catherine smiled.

Life couldn't possibly get any sweeter, could it?

1

A DAY TO REMEMBER

Two Days Later

lackness engulfed him, and William strained his ears as distant voices spoke nearby. His limbs felt strangely heavy, and his head pounded, a dull ache pulsing behind his forehead.

With all his might, he tried to push back the heavy fog that rested on his mind, but it weighed him down like iron shackles.

"Go and rest," a voice said, sounding kind but commanding. "You've been sitting with him all day. I promise I will send for you the moment he comes to."

William frowned. *His brother. It was his brother's voice. Who was he talking to?*

A door opened and then closed, and for a moment, William wondered if he was alone.

Then footsteps echoed to his ears as well as the sound of a chair being dragged forward, its legs scarping over the soft rug.

Once more, William tried to clear his mind, trying to remember what had happened. How had he gotten back to the house? And why was his brother sitting by his bed?

Willing his eyes to open, William moaned when the soft light from the candle on the nightstand pierced his eyes painfully.

"Will?" Grabbing his hand, his brother shot to his feet and the chair toppled over and clattered to the floor. "Will, can you hear me?"

Blinking, William tried to focus his gaze, and slowly, ever so slowly, his brother's face came into focus. "Wesley?" he whispered. "What happened?"

For a moment, his brother's eyes closed, and utter relief washed over his face before he took a deep breath and met William's eyes. "Do you not remember?"

William frowned, then glanced around. "Am I at Harrington Park?"

Wesley nodded. "You had an accident. We went out on horseback." Guilt on his face, he shook his head as his lips pressed into a thin line. "Maybe we shouldn't have. The snow was too deep." He swallowed, then took a deep breath and pressed on. "Your horse stumbled over a root or something hidden in the snow, and you were thrown. You rolled down the small slope and fell into the lake, breaking through the thin layer of ice."

Listening, William could not recall the events his brother was recounting with a most painful expression on his face. Why could he not remember?

Rubbing his hands over his face, Wesley gritted his teeth. "When you didn't come back up and sank under the surface, I thought…" Shaking his head, he took a deep breath. "You must've hit your head and lost consciousness. You almost drowned."

"And you pulled me out?" William asked.

"I did."

"I thank you for that, Brother."

A soft smile on his lips, Wesley shook his head. "Ever the charmer." Then he laughed and once more rubbed his hands over his face as though trying to rid himself of the memories that William eluded.

Looking up at his brother, William frowned. "Did you get hurt as well?"

"Me? No, why do you ask?"

"Where did you get that scar on your left cheek?" The moment the question left his lips William realised that the injury that had left the scar had to have occurred some time ago. Then his mind found another oddity that had eluded him before. "Snow? Did you say there was snow?" Frowning, he stared at his brother. "Why would there be snow in May?"

Wesley's eyes opened wide. "It's November."

"What?" William swallowed as the world slowly turned upside down. Staring at his brother's face, he thought this had to be a joke, and yet, Wesley had never seemed farther from joking than he did in that moment. "How can it be November?" he stammered, unable to express the confusion that coursed through his head as he tried to make sense of his brother's words. "Are you certain?"

Wesley nodded, concern creasing his forehead. "I am." He swallowed. "What is the last thing you remember? What is the last date you remember?"

William closed his eyes, trying to drag up the images that hovered nearby. "The ball at Westington's. When was that? May 8th?" His eyes snapped up to meet his brother's. "How long have I been in this bed?"

"Two days," Wesley whispered, shaking his head as though he, too, could not believe what was happening. "You've been asleep for two days, and today, it's Sunday, November 29."

Rubbing his hands over his face, William thought this had to be a bad dream. How could he not remember the last few months of his life? Again, he turned to his brother. "What happened since then? When did you get that scar? I don't remember anything."

Wesley frowned, and absentmindedly he brushed a finger down the thin scar that ran over his left cheek. "It was a fencing accident. The blossom came off, and we didn't notice."

"We?" William asked, and a new cold spread through his body as he saw his brother's expression.

Wesley nodded. "It was your foil," he whispered as though afraid to speak too loudly. "But that was four years ago."

Again, William's eyes went wide, and he felt as though someone was sitting on his chest, squeezing the air from his lungs.

"You said that the last date that you remember," Wesley began, "was May 8th." Nodding, William stared at his brother, who swallowed and then took a deep breath before continuing. "What year was that?"

For a moment, William had no idea what his brother was asking before the realisation of its implications hit him right in the chest, squeezing the remaining air from his lungs. Gasping for breath, he closed his eyes as bright spots began to dance in his field of vision.

"What year, Will?"

William opened his eyes and met his brother's gaze. "1813."

Wesley swallowed. "That was five years ago. It's now 1818." Picking up the chair that had toppled over, his brother slumped into it as though unable to keep upright. "How is this possible?" he asked, his eyes distant for a second before they returned to William. "Do you truly not remember anything beyond May 8th, 1813?"

Raking his mind, William tried to find something that he could place at a later date with certainty, but there was nothing. As though the fall had knocked them out of his head, five years had vanished into oblivion. Were they gone for good? William wondered, fear clawing at his heart. "What don't I remember?" he whispered, meeting his brother's eyes. "Mother, is she all right?"

Wesley nodded, and William exhaled the breath that he'd been holding.

"What else?" he pressed, unwilling to draw out the inevitable. Whatever he had experienced, lived through the past five years would now find him unprepared and unknowing. "Tell me what I don't know."

For a split second, Wesley's eyes widened before he turned them to his brother once more. "There is something that you need to know."

He swallowed, and William steeled himself for the shock that awaited him. Who had died? What loss had he forgotten?

Leaning forward, Wesley took his brother's hand. "You're married," he whispered, his eyes searching William's face.

As he was expecting to hear that someone close to him had passed away, relief filled William's heart and he smiled, inhaling deeply.

"Do you remember her?" Wesley asked, hope ringing in his voice.

Instantly, relief was replaced by panic, and William stared at his brother, shaking his head.

Sadness darkened his brother's features. "Her name is Catherine, Catherine Dansby. Well, that was her name. Now, she is Catherine Everett, Countess of Harrington." The hint of a wistful smile came to Wesley's face. "You met her about two years ago, and from the moment you laid eyes on her, you were lost. You both were." He chuckled. "Honestly, Brother, I've never seen you so besotted with a woman. You've been married for a year now, and you still look at each other the same way you did then."

Closing his eyes, William sighed.

"Do you truly not remember her?" his brother asked. "Nothing? Nothing at all?"

Meeting Wesley's hopeful eyes, William shook his head.

"Well, maybe you'll recognise her once you see her," he said, his voice, however, sounded feeble, and the doubt that rang in it sent chills down William's back. "She's been sitting here with you for two days. Only minutes before you woke up, I sent her to her room to rest." He swallowed. "But I promised to send for her the minute you woke up."

A question hung in the air, and a part of William wanted to ignore it. What if he saw her and didn't remember her? What would he do then?

There was nothing he could do. Whether he remembered his wife—*his wife!*—or not, they were tied to each other! For better or worse, wasn't that what it said?

"Send for her," William whispered, knowing that no matter what, he could not run from this moment forever.

Blinking, Catherine yawned as her maid gently shook her shoulder, calling her name. For a moment, everything seemed distant and her mind felt heavy with sleep. But then her memories returned, and her eyes flew open. "My husband?" she gasped, staring at Sally's face as her heart hammered in her chest.

"He woke up," her maid whispered, a joyous smile on her face.

For a second, Catherine's heart stopped. Then she jumped to her feet, all fatigue falling from her limbs as she raced out of her bedchamber and down the corridor. Unable to slow herself, she burst through the door into her husband's chamber.

Startled, her brother-in-law spun around and the chair he'd sat on clattered to the floor once again. "Catherine," he gasped, his eyes guarded, his shoulders tense as though he had just received bad news.

Trying to catch her breath, Catherine pushed past him, her eyes searching for the man in the bed. Had something happened? Had he taken a turn for the worse?

Relief washed over her when she found her husband lying in bed, his eyes open, his chest rising and falling with every precious breath. "William," she whispered, and tears flooded her eyes and spilled down her cheeks. "I was so afraid."

"Hello," he whispered, his eyes searching her face.

Sinking onto the bed next to her husband, Catherine took his hand, feeling the warmth of his skin, and all the strains of the past two days fell from her. Whatever had happened didn't matter. The only thing that mattered was that he had returned to her.

Holding his hand against her cheek, she sat by his side as she had for the past two days, only now the tears that spilled down her face were tears of joy. Gazing down at him, she smiled. "I was so afraid to lose you, William. I don't know what I would do without you."

Averting his gaze, he swallowed. "I...eh..." His gaze shifted upward and past her shoulder.

"Is something wrong?" Catherine asked, seeing the strain on his face. "Are you in pain?" Turning her head, she looked up at her brother-in-law. "Wesley, we should call Dr. Martin."

Stepping forward, his face grave, her brother-in-law placed a hand on her shoulder. "Not yet."

As fear crept up her spine, Catherine's gaze travelled back and forth between the two brothers. Something was wrong. She could see it in their eyes. "What is it? Will you not tell me?"

Wesley nodded before he once more turned to his brother. "Are you certain?" he asked. "Nothing at all?"

In reply, William shook his head, unable to meet her eyes. "I'm sorry."

"What?" Catherine asked, fear pressing on her heart. "Tell me!"

Wesley took a deep breath and turned to her. "William seems fine...physically fine although I will send for Dr. Martin to be certain. However," again, he took a deep breath, and chills crawled up Catherine's arms, "he seems to be suffering from...memory loss."

"Memory loss?" Catherine's eyes went wide before she turned to her husband. "William?"

"I'm sorry," he whispered, his gaze barely meeting hers.

At his words, a new cold spread through Catherine's heart, and her mind felt dizzy and confused. "What are you...?" She swallowed, trying to focus her thoughts. "Are you saying you...you don't remember me?"

Almost helpless, he lay there, his eyes clouded and distant, as Catherine's heart broke into a million little pieces. "That cannot be so," she whispered. "I'm your wife. I..." A spark of hope swelled in her chest, and she said the only words that would convince her, "William, you're impossible." She had meant to say them lightly, but her voice broke on the last word.

As fresh tears streamed down her face, she sat by his side and waited, hoping beyond hope to hear the words that would mean she hadn't lost him.

However, he did not say them.

"I apologise," he whispered instead, his face holding guilt and remorse above any other emotion she had hoped to see there. "I don't know what to say. The last thing I want is to cause you pain, but I cannot give you what I don't have."

As her hands began to tremble, she released his. No longer was he the man she loved, the man who loved her. From one moment to the next, he had become a stranger, just as she was to him, and oddly enough, holding hands seemed far too intimate. Inappropriate even.

Dazed, Catherine rose to her feet, her hands smoothing down her dress before they began to tremble once more. Unable to keep them still, she laced her fingers, her nails digging painfully into the back of her hands. "I need to go," she whispered, and before either of the two men could reply, she spun around and fled the room.

LOVE'S SECOND CHANCE SERIES

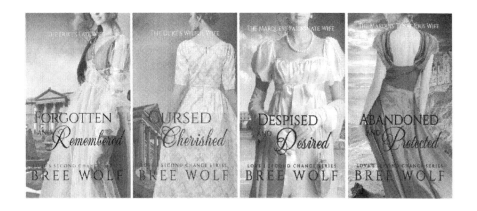

A FORBIDDEN LOVE
NOVELLA SERIES

For more information, visit

www.breewolf.com

Printed in Great Britain
by Amazon